THE WORLD
BETWEEN US

RUTH MADISON

To get bonus scenes, stories, character art, and other extra content, visit my website at

https://ruthmadisonbooks.com/bonus

CONTENTS

—·—

OTHER BOOKS BY RUTH MADISON

The Unbroken Novella Series

(On Kindle Unlimited)

love that won't quit even when the body does

The Billionaire's Secretary

Wheely Into You

Stand Alone And Other

The World Between Us

Out Of Water

Waiting To Break

(W)hole

Breath(ε)

Sled Hockey Team Of Cedar Harbor Series

Thawing An Ice Heart

Saving His Soulmate

Hearts Unmasked

Love Comes Back

Get Bonus Content For All Books At: https://ruthmad

isonbooks.com/bonus

1

S tephanie's phone buzzed inside her purse and she kicked it further under her desk without looking. Betsy, whose desk was across from hers, raised an eyebrow but said nothing.

Stephanie should have been proofreading her RFP report one more time but she was too anxious about it. It was good enough. It would have to be good enough. She had been working on it non-stop for a week.

To calm her nerves she was scrolling her favorite music news website. In her spare time Stephanie had started a YouTube channel dedicated to the local music scene and working on that gave her a lot more satisfaction than writing grants and proposals. Then an unexpected headline on a blog caught her eye and she sat up straighter. "No way," she murmured to herself.

Just as she clicked to read the full article Betsy hissed, "Here he comes."

Stephanie looked up and saw their supervisor heading down the hall towards them. This was her chance. *Stand up and stand out,* she repeated her father's mantra in her head, *Stand up and stand out.* She closed down the window on her computer, grabbed her RFP draft, and hurried to meet his stride.

"Mr. Bolan, this is—"

"What are you wearing?" he interrupted. They both stopped walking and he looked at her sternly.

"Excuse me?" Stephanie said. This conversation was already taking a turn into unexpected territory.

"Your pants," Mr. Bolan said.

"My pants?" She looked down at her favorite power pants. She had spent $70 on them, more than she had spent on any piece of clothing that wasn't a winter coat. They were a subtle pinstripe of light gray against dark gray and they made her feel confident and powerful. She wore them every time she needed a boost.

"That's a pattern and it's against the dress code."

Stephanie stared at him. To call a very professional gray-on-gray pinstripe a pattern seemed an outrageous overstatement but the last time Stephanie had contradicted Bolan it had not ended well.

"I'm going to have to write you up."

Stephanie stayed rooted to the spot unable to say anything. She wanted to beg him not to. She wanted to tell him to just focus on her report. Why did anything other than the RFP draft matter?

He was already walking away.

She knew he was spreading rumors that she was not following directions and he questioned her qualifications to his supervisors. Now instead of getting to take the lead on a proposal she was getting written up for her most expensive and professional pair of pants. Couldn't make this shit up.

She walked back to her desk and dropped into her chair with a sigh.

"How did it go?" Betsy asked. "Did he like your proposal?"

Stephanie sunk her head onto her arms on the desk. "He didn't look at it," she said. "I'm never going to get ahead here."

"That man is the worst," Betsy huffed. But the truth was she never did more than make disapproving noises. Stephanie was on her own in this mess. It wasn't like she hadn't known she would be when she took the job even after seeing that there were no other people of color on the team.

This was killing her. Her parents had encouraged her to take the job. They were certain she could prove herself even if she had to work five times harder than everyone else. And she had tried. For years she had tried her hardest. And the job had worn her down. Did she even want to prove herself here anymore? Did she want to be writing proposals and grants for the rest of her life?

What she really wanted to do was grow her side hustle into a full time job and prove to her family that she could use creativity to get ahead too. She could do things her way, not theirs, and still succeed.

That reminded her of the article she had started to click on and her mood lifted as she clicked the window back open. David Sinclair was arriving back in town after a two year tour.

David Sinclair had become a huge international rock star, but he grew up here. He was the only famous resident and the city cashed in on that as much as possible. And now he was coming back home. Was there any chance she could get him on her channel? That would be huge. Even her parents would have to acknowledge her music journalism career could be legit.

He had actually been discovered on YouTube himself, though it was several years ago. Maybe he would be sympathetic to someone trying to get a foothold there.

No point in polishing this RFP now anyway, may as well dig into learning about David Sinclair. Stephanie had heard his music on the radio, of course, but she didn't know much about his personal life.

Stephanie's phone buzzed for the third time that afternoon and she ignored it. This time Betsy said, "Not going to answer?"

Stephanie almost lied and said it was a spam call but Betsy was a friend. "It's Marcus," she said.

"Oh! Does he want to apologize?"

"I don't know about that but he does want to get back together."

"And?"

"I don't want to think about it," Stephanie muttered. The truth was she was considering it. Everyone in her life thought the breakup was insanity. She scrolled further on the blog but this article was brief, focused only on David returning home. "Hey, Betsy, what do you know about David Sinclair?"

"Oh my God he is so hot." She pretended to fan herself and giggled. "I used to know someone who went to elementary school with him."

"Used to?"

"Drug overdose," Betsy said way too blithely.

"Oh. Um, I'm sorry."

"It's kind of a miracle David got out of that neighborhood. He might be the only success story they've ever had."

Stephanie blinked. Yikes. In theory she knew there were some pockets of extreme poverty and drug issues in the city but she had never been personally touched by it. Her parents had a determination to not be associated with "those kind of Blacks." Stephanie was beginning to suspect that the difference between them was little more than luck, timing, and opportunity, though.

Now she was even more curious about David, but she had a meeting to get to in a few minutes. She stood up and tried not to think about her pants, but the whole walk to the meeting room she felt like all eyes were on them even though that was objectively ridiculous. So much for them bringing her confidence, these pants were ruined for good. She couldn't wait for this day to be over and to get home to her happy little apartment.

After the meeting, she stopped back at her desk just long enough to grab her purse and head for the door. She passed by most of the cars in the parking lot until she got to her powder blue beach cruiser bicycle. Her brother, Adam, always rolled his eyes about the bike and told her only white people could be hipsters but she didn't care, she loved her bicycle. She put her purse into a backpack and pushed off towards the grocery store for something resembling dinner.

While there she took the opportunity to grab a magazine with a cover story about David Sinclair. She stuffed everything into her backpack and hopped onto her bike for the ride to her apartment. It was in an old stone building that looked a little bit worse for wear but the inside was much nicer than you would think from the outside. She pushed her bike up the ramp to the side of the stairs, chained it in the lobby, and climbed the stairs to the second floor, sliding her hand along the smooth wrought-iron railing.

Stephanie absolutely loved her apartment. It was the first home she had picked out for herself and everything about it was just for her. The huge round yellow rug on top of the beige carpet, her bed against the right wall with a sunflower comforter and extra pillows. Her desk was along the far wall where she could see out the window while she edited videos.

The mini fridge was in the far left corner and she put away her groceries, took off the offending pants, then put sliced cheese on bread and climbed onto her bed to eat it with the magazine spread in front of her. She flipped straight to the article about David.

First the picture. Cheeky grin, white skin with a peachy undertone, tousled dark brown hair, a twinkle in his eye. She had seen him before but took more time now to look him over. There was something about his expression that invited you forward, teased you with the idea that there was something special he wanted to share with just you. One thing was certain, David Sinclair had charisma in spades.

She perused the article carefully. She knew he had gotten his start on YouTube just like her. Well, okay, he had made it a bit further than she (so far). It was eight years ago that David first burst on the scene with his mysterious YouTube videos. Dark and artfully shadowed, they allowed people to focus purely on the music. Music that was soulful and deeply emotional. A throwback in many ways to the alt rock of the 90s (her own personal favorite genre).

Eventually the article continued on to his home life, explaining that he and his handicapped younger brother were raised by a single mother in the poorest part of the city. His success had been critical in saving his family and getting his brother much needed care and medical equipment. Now the mentally handicapped, wheelchair-bound brother traveled with David. Stephanie had never heard anything so sweet.

David Sinclair was a conundrum. He was known for his hard partying and devil-may-care attitude yet he continued to care for his vulnerable little brother. This was definitely a story worth pursuing for her channel. It could even be the break that could propel her to another level. It could be her ticket out of her job. Now she just had to maneuver a way to meet him.

2

I t was past midnight when the tour bus finally pulled into David's driveway, the sky inky dark without even a star visible. A few hours earlier the atmosphere on the bus had been upbeat and raucous but the excitement of returning home had dissipated and now everyone was unnaturally quiet. Shawn snored lightly in one row. David was looking at his phone, the glow of the screen reflecting into his eyes. Dylan couldn't quite put his finger on what he was feeling but it was probably the same for his brother. They had been out on tour for two years and now it was over for the time being. One final homecoming concert and then a break. What was their life without the speed and pressure of performance?

Coming back home was something they had looked forward to. They had planned out and built their two houses next door to each other. But was it really home when they had never lived in these houses? They weren't returning to the neighborhood they had left from two years ago. That would never be their home again. Which was a good thing. So why did he feel so odd?

The bus groaned to a stop and David slapped his bandmates on the shoulders as he walked down the aisle to exit. He shook Shawn awake and Dylan watched as they exchanged an old handshake from their childhood.

Dylan slid his body across the plush seat to his wheelchair and waited for the lift to slowly whir out of the side of the bus. By the time he was exiting onto the asphalt driveway he could see his mother in the doorway of David's house. Her straw-colored hair was pulled back into a thin ponytail. The light from the house behind her illuminated stark shadows on her face.

David kissed her cheek and walked past her into the house. Dylan's custom-built home was next door but he headed for David's door instead. His mother's eyes crinkled as she smiled and bent down to wrap a thin arm over his shoulders.

"Hi, mom," he said.

"Hey, sweetie," she said. The smell of cigarettes wafted off her and clogged the air around him. There was a worn quality to her smile and Dylan noted the deep lines and bags under her eyes. He caught David's eye behind his mother's back and the look that passed between them told him his brother had also noticed the signs that she was using again.

"Let's all get some rest," Dylan said, pushing against his smooth metal pushrims and into David's house. It hadn't escaped his notice that David had made his own home wheelchair accessible and created a first-floor suite for any time Dylan wanted to stay over. The amount of time they spent together might be codependent but they had always had only each other to rely on.

David dropped his messenger bag on a chair and bounded up the stairs two at a time, quickly disappearing around a corner. Their mother followed Dylan down the hall to his room. He noted that she had already put fresh sheets on the bed and there was a glass of water on the bed-side table.

"Thanks, mom," Dylan said.

She stayed leaning against the doorframe. "Do you need any help?"

"No, I got it," Dylan said, "Why don't you head to bed?"

"Okay," she said. "My phone is on, so text if you need me."

"Will do." No need to mention that he had been getting on fine for years without her being around. She wanted to feel useful and she hardly knew what to do with herself now that she didn't have to work herself to the bone. He and David had wanted to make her life easier but she probably needed a hobby to fill her days.

She drifted away from the door as quiet as a ghost.

Once she had left, Dylan turned to the bathroom so he could get ready to sleep. He was exhausted and it would be nice to just pee and collapse into bed but nothing was ever going to be that simple for his paralyzed body.

It took about thirty minutes to get through his night routine in record time and he gratefully pulled up to the bed, peeled back the cover, and lifted his body onto the crisp, clean sheets. There would be no rest tomorrow, they would be busy setting up for the homecoming concert and probably looking at a rehab facility for mom.

As difficult as it was to try to keep her clean, he had to be grateful that they had the resources to help her. One of these days she would recover and go back to being the woman David had told him about over the years, the happy and content mother Dylan had never known. He had to believe that it was possible to give her back what she had lost when he was born.

3

Stephanie checked the time on her phone. Better get ready for her usual Tuesday night filming of open mic night at her friend's bar. She put on jeans and a Killers tour t-shirt, splashed water on her face, and scrunched her fingers against her scalp to revive her curls. Grabbing her camera bag she was back out the door thirty minutes after she got home from work.

She lived in a building that wasn't technically in the city but was close enough that she could walk or bike most places. And she loved riding around town with the air on her face. Still, in the evenings she preferred to drive for safety so she passed by her bicycle in the lobby and headed to her little red car in the garage at the back. It was a used car and was coming up on 17 years old. Still going strong.

She arrived early enough there was still street parking. Chance's open mic night was gaining in popularity, in part because of her channel.

"Hey, Chance" she greeted him as she dropped her bag on a bar stool. White parents certainly could compete in the weird name game. She would have thought Chance was a dog's name. "Did you hear David Sinclair is coming back home?"

"He's already here," Chance said, not pausing from wiping glasses dry. "They're setting up tonight at the dome. Concert's on Saturday."

"Tonight?" Stephanie stared at him.

"Yeah, they're there tonight."

Stephanie looked at the stage even though open mic hadn't started yet. She was torn. Did she keep up with her usual schedule of showcasing local up and comers or did she head for the dome and try to get in front of David Sinclair?

The risk was she might have no footage for her channel but she was in a plateau. She needed something to give her a boost to the next level. Just one really viral video could get her to where she could actually justify YouTube as a career.

Besides, how could she pass up even the slightest chance to be in front of David Sinclair? Why was she even debating this? She had to go for it.

"I'm gonna go see if I can catch him," she said to Chance. She was out the door with her bag before he could reply.

The drive to the dome was not as easy. She had to navigate some complex streets but she had been there enough times she didn't need to put on GPS. Every moment she got closer her stomach tightened a little more. She couldn't deny she was nervous. David was a big deal.

By the time the dome was in view she still had no idea what she was going to say to him. Assuming she could even get in front of him. This was the boldest thing she had ever done for her channel. She was making decisions so fast her brain couldn't even catch up.

There was no show tonight so, as she got closer, the dome was not lit up and traffic was sparse. She took the final turn. No turning back, she muttered to herself. This could be it, the moment that would change her life forever. *Time to be bold, Stephanie, you got this. Stand up and stand out.*

The parking lot at the dome was emptier than Stephanie had ever seen it. She parked next to two vans with their back doors open. Before she got out she typed a quick post for the community tab of her channel. "David Sinclair has returned home and tonight he's getting set up for a homecoming concert on Saturday. Leave a comment if you're hearing about this here first! I don't know whether he'll be here tonight but we're going to go check it out."

She dropped the phone in her pocket and headed for the open vans. It was simple enough to grab a piece of equipment and start helping with the unloading. She didn't have the same color shirt as the other people unloading but no one paid her any attention.

Inside the building she carried a mess of cords towards the stage where several people bustled, moving things here and there. As she hoped, David was there. He was standing just below the stage surrounded by a small knot of people discussing something that seemed logistical.

At first she didn't notice but the little brother was there too. She wondered if he literally went everywhere with David.

Once she saw him, it was hard to look away. There was something so off about him that her brain struggled to process and put him into place. He was strangely tiny. In his wheelchair the top of his head reached about to David's belly button.

His face was very like David's. Same brown hair with a slight wave, same dark brown eyes, same light skin. He wore baggy jeans that bunched up everywhere on his obviously thin legs, a t-shirt that pooled in his lap, and a leather jacket. His body sank deeply into a thick cushion on the wheelchair's seat, the fabric encroaching around his thighs. Puffy white sneakers without laces hovered above the ground on some kind of bar for his feet.

But not only was he small, he also wasn't proportional. His chest was so truncated it was as though someone had removed a cross section and attached his chest at the nipples directly to his hips. His shoulders were broad and thick. With the missing part of his midsection, his arms seemed outrageously long and he also leaned towards his right side.

And then Stephanie realized that the brother was looking at her. Everyone had fallen quiet and even David and his entourage were watching her.

"I'm sorry," she murmured, almost tripping as she rushed to put the cords onto the stage.

"You get a good look?" David asked, his tone icy and his eyes boring into her.

"I didn't mean any harm," she said, feeling her chest tightening with embarrassment.

The brother smiled then and his smile was so different from David's that they no longer looked at all alike. Where David's smile was impish, his brother's was deeply sincere. Just looking into his face, warmth spread through Stephanie's body and she felt herself relaxing despite the circumstances.

"It's no problem," he said. "I'm Dylan."

Stephanie was so startled that she said without thinking, "You can understand?"

At that moment laughter exploded around her. David slapped his thigh and tears gathered at the corners of his eyes.

Dylan rolled his eyes and muttered to David, "I hope you're pleased with yourself."

"Man," David said, "It makes a great story. Rich and famous David Sinclair takes care of his poor retarded brother."

Dylan elbowed him in the knee. "Would you stop saying that word? Jeez, David."

"Hey," David said, "What's good for the David Sinclair image is good for all of us. And people are eating it up!"

"You're not...mentally challenged, are you?" Stephanie said.

"No," Dylan said. "But the idea seems to be quite compelling."

Stephanie fumbled in her pocket for her phone. "I could set the record straight," she said.

"Are you a reporter?" David asked sharply.

"Sort of. I do a YouTube channel about music and music news."

"Put it away," David said. "No interviews."

"I'm sorry," Stephanie said and began to retreat back towards the door. "I shouldn't have come."

Panic was welling up in her stomach and climbing towards her throat. This was crazy. Why had she done this? Could she ever really be a successful YouTube journalist if she couldn't handle this? Was her entire future career plan going to fall apart right here and now tonight?

"Wait," Dylan said.

David gave him a look but he ignored it. "You're local, yeah?" Dylan said to Stephanie.

She nodded.

"We've been away for a while and we don't know the current hot places. David wants to hit up the best club tonight. Would you know which one is the best? I'm thinking you've got some expertise in that area."

Stephanie nodded. "Yeah, I could help you with that."

"Okay," Dylan said. "When we're finished here, stick around. You can tag along. But no filming."

Stephanie nodded again. "Okay."

She went back to helping with the equipment set up until she heard David say, "I'm bored. Let's get out of here."

He headed for the door immediately and left the planning to others.

Dylan flagged her over. "What was your name?" he asked.

"I'm Stephanie," she said.

"Awesome," Dylan said. "Where are we going?"

"Definitely Coco Kitty," Stephanie said without hesitation.

Dylan nodded. "I know the place," he said. "We'll meet you there."

Stephanie stood rooted to the spot for several moments watching as Dylan gripped smooth metal rails on the wheels of his chair and glided easily across the wood floor. His motions with the wheelchair were so fluid it was as though the chair were a natural extension of his body. Even while he moved, though, the top of his body still listed to the right. Perhaps he couldn't sit straight.

"You coming?" he called over his shoulder and Stephanie gave herself a shake to break the spell. She followed out the door and into the parking lot.

In her car she pulled out her phone to record a brief segment to be edited into a full video later. "I've lucked out, friends," she told the camera. "Met

David Sinclair face to face and now I'm heading to the Coco Kitty with him. I'll see if I can get a shot with him."

While she spoke she watched a lift slowly grind out and down from the side of a small van and Dylan pushed his wheelchair up onto it. She looked away before he could catch her staring again.

***

At the club there were already crowds. When she got out of her car, Dylan waved her over and— along with the rest of David's group—they bypassed the line. Dylan was just ahead of Stephanie and she was looking directly down at the top of his head when he stopped short and she almost tripped over him. There was a lip up into the club that Stephanie had never noticed. Before she could ask if he needed help, though, he had expertly popped up onto his back wheels and lifted the small front wheels onto the top of the lip. He gave one hard push and he was up over the ledge. Clearly he knew what he was doing with the wheelchair.

Immediately David vanished into the VIP area and Stephanie hurried to keep up with him. He bounded up a spiral staircase of clear plastic steps and behind a curtain. Stephanie was close behind. Without filming she wasn't sure what her YouTube video about this would be but she needed to stick close to him to make sure she got some kind of story out of the evening.

Quickly Stephanie found herself bored. She sat on a stiff velvet sofa across from where David was laughing and drinking and yelling and pawing at girls. David had entirely ignored her and his behavior was nothing special to note. He was like so many of the men Stephanie had gone out clubbing with. Self-absorbed, loud, demanding, and obnoxious.

As if on cue, her phone buzzed with a text from Marcus. She sent off a quick message that she was busy working (even though he didn't think her YouTube channel was work). She wasn't surprised when he texted again but she ignored it. He was going to be so pissed when she finally got back to him. Not that she owed him anything. He was an ex, after all.

It was a long time before she realized that Dylan was not with the rest of the group. She hadn't thought about it as she had climbed the long spiral staircase that he wasn't going to follow them up to the VIP lounge. Since David wasn't doing anything at all unique or interesting Stephanie wandered back out from behind the curtain and stood along the railing next to the staircase looking down. The whole floor shook with the pounding of the music. She filmed the crowds for a few moments.

Despite his small stature it didn't take long to notice Dylan with the unique movement of his wheelchair. He was skirting the edge of the floor and heading towards the exit. Stephanie gave a quick glance behind her but she had a much better chance of getting a story from Dylan than from David so she gently pushed her way down the packed stairway and followed toward the door.

Outside the air was much cooler and her ears vibrated from the sudden quiet. It wasn't quite raining but there was a damp mist in the air. She saw Dylan sitting by the edge of the curb a few yards from the door and she walked that way.

"Out for a smoke?" she asked.

He looked up at her, surprised. Then he smiled and said, "No, I don't smoke."

"May I join you?" she asked.

Before she could sit on the curb beside him he said, "Hold on."

He peeled off his leather jacket, revealing a Greenday t-shirt and surprisingly muscular arms. (Although maybe it shouldn't surprise her. He did use his arms as a substitute for his legs, after all.) Then he laid the jacket out on the sidewalk where she was about to sit.

"Thank you," Stephanie said, truly touched. She sat down on his jacket and at that point they were almost eye to eye, he just slightly above her.

"So if you don't smoke what are you doing out here?" Stephanie said.

He looked at her for a moment, considering. Eventually he said, "This is going to sound stupid."

Stephanie shook her head. "I'm sure it won't," she said.

"The truth is I hate being in crowded places like this. I'm always afraid I'll get trampled."

Stephanie considered his petite frame. "Makes sense," she said.

They sat quietly side by side for a while watching drunk friends stumble across the street together. Then Dylan said, "YouTube, huh?"

"Yeah," Stephanie said.

"How is it going?"

"Not bad," she said. "I'm really close to being able to make it a full time career. That's how David started, right?"

Dylan nodded. "It was easier back then," he said. "A lot less competition. These days YouTube is full of musicians with a ton of talent."

"Could I record you for a moment? Just telling something about David?"

"No, I'd rather not."

"Okay."

They were quiet for a few more moments listening to the heavy bass of the club music vibrating from behind them.

Then Stephanie asked, "What's your favorite kind of music?"

"Tough question. I guess I would have to say classic rock and 90s alternative."

Stephanie smiled. "Angsty white boys. Me too," she said.

"Really?"

"Don't look so surprised. What, I'm only allowed to like gangster rap?" She raised her eyebrows.

"That's not what I meant," Dylan protested, throwing up his hands.

"Isn't it?" Stephanie challenged.

He thought for a moment, returning his hands to his lap, elbows on the tops of his wheels. "Yeah, okay, I guess I was being racist."

"Happens to the best of us," Stephanie said with a forgiving smile.

"Ableism too," Dylan said.

Stephanie considered this. She had never before thought about the ways that people were prejudiced against disabled people. "Guilty as charged," she said.

She looked down at his sneakers with the tongues pushed out and no laces. They would fall right off if he were walking in them. In fact, the style was from at least five years ago but the shoes were still pristine white.

"So what's the weirdest thing someone's ever said to you?" he asked. She looked back up at his face and he grinned at her.

"How can I pick just one? How about 'I don't usually like Black girls but you're giving me jungle fever.'"

"Ouch." Dylan paused then said, "'If you believed in Jesus he would cure you and you could walk.'"

"Wow. Okay. I'm breaking out the YouTube comments."

"Oh no! Anything but that. Are YouTube commenters even human?"

"It would be hard to tell."

"I used to see David's but at least those criticisms were based on music, not racist or sexist."

"Okay if we leave out the Internet, people touching my hair without asking."

"People pushing my chair to 'help' without asking. It's well-meaning and also dangerous."

Stephanie's chest tightened at the thought of people manhandling Dylan and endangering him while trying to be good samaritans. But she didn't want to end the game so she said, "How about, 'I'm scared of getting pulled over too.'"

"You got a license for that thing?" Dylan returned with a crooked smile.

"No! People do not say that!"

Then they were both laughing so hard they could barely take a breath. Stephanie had never laughed about all the racist things she'd heard and yet Dylan was making it almost...fun? She felt so relaxed and she couldn't remember the last time she had been so free around someone else.

Even when she was with Marcus she always felt at least a little bit guarded and the need to say the right thing...be the right thing. How was it she felt so relaxed sitting with a disabled white boy? Was it just that his wheelchair made him feel safe to be around?

They continued to talk, mostly about music, and the conversation flowed easily.

It was last call when David came stumbling out of the club with the rest of their crew. He was a wrecking ball to the delicate bubble that she and Dylan had been existing in, oblivious to anyone outside himself.

"There you are!" David tumbled towards Dylan and slapped his shoulder. "Let's go."

Dylan gave Stephanie an apologetic smile and held out his hand to help her up. She reached out for his fingers and found his hand rough and strong. Once she had hoisted herself to her feet she lifted his jacket. "It's damp," she said.

"No problem," Dylan said. He laid the jacket across his lap. "I won't feel it anyway."

Before Stephanie could ask what that meant, he was following David and crew. His triceps flexed as he propelled the wheelchair. Stephanie watched, transfixed.

It wasn't until they were out of sight that his spell over her broke and Stephanie went back to her car and then her quiet apartment, feeling a strange let down from the evening.

It was like there was some kind of electric charge between her and Dylan...but that was ridiculous. It wasn't like she could be attracted to someone like him. She laughed at the thought. "You need to get more sleep, Stephanie," she mumbled out loud to herself.

Though it was 3:00 am when she got back and there was work in the morning she still spent an hour putting together what little footage she had into a story and got her video uploaded. The YouTube grind was relentless, at least at this stage.

When she finally collapsed into bed she fell asleep thinking of the warm feeling of sitting next to Dylan on the sidewalk.

4

D ylan followed along behind David, quiet as usual. There was no
reason for David to notice the conflict raging in Dylan. Internally
he cursed himself for the crush he was already developing on this woman
who had paid him a modicum of attention. At best she was just being nice
to him. At worst she was using him to get closer to David.

He looked up at his handsome and charming brother a few paces ahead,
laughing and rating the girls he had met that night while leaning against
Keenan. Stephanie hadn't even registered a blip on David's radar, though
Dylan couldn't figure out why. She was stunning and far more intelligent
than most of the women who ended up in their circle. Hmmm that might
be his answer right there.

But whatever the reason Stephanie had spent time with him, it wasn't
so she could have a disabled guy pining for her. That was never the reason
Dylan had discovered from experience.

"Dude, get a move on," David complained as Dylan lagged behind.
Dylan didn't say anything but he gave his wheels a hard push and caught
up, feeling the cold metal rims chilled by the night air sliding by under his
fingers. He couldn't wait to get home and try to forget Stephanie and this
whole magical night.

It was easier when the beautiful women ignored him. Just enjoy the experience for what it was, he admonished himself. It was a special moment and he could treasure having experienced it. He took in a deep breath. The moist air carried the city smells of gasoline and street food. It was nice being back in familiar territory after so long away.

David was stumbling and lay his hand on Dylan's shoulder to steady himself. Even though David rarely drank to the point of throwing up anymore, he did drink to a point Dylan seriously wondered if David could use a wheelchair too. It was weird watching abled people struggle to stand. Dylan had never stood or walked in his life so he didn't know what it was like. He very rarely thought about it except on nights like this.

It was difficult to move with David leaning on him. Keenan noticed and took over, looping David's arm over his shoulder and gently guiding him off Dylan. David seemed entirely unaware of his surroundings.

They arrived at their white van and the other guys all piled in while Dylan waited for one of them to lower the lift. It was a van they mostly used for the music equipment but they fitted it with a lift for convenience. It wasn't that Dylan couldn't get in a regular car but sometimes it was just simpler to transport him like equipment.

He chided himself for being bitter. It didn't help anything. The feelings Stephanie had awakened in him were going to be hard to put to rest. It reminded him of high school when he thought Jane Boer liked him. She came over to watch The Princess Bride (yes, he had his own copy, don't judge).

He had moved from his wheelchair onto the sofa beside her and she had eagerly whispered, "What can you tell me about David? What kind of girls does he like?"

It was the first but not the last time a woman had shown interest in him just to get closer to his brother. And Stephanie had even more reason to do just that.

Dylan rumbled onto the metal lift and rode it up to the van. Thankfully Shawn was used to being the designated driver. Dylan didn't tend to drink much since coordination was pretty important for using a wheelchair but he also had never learned to drive. It's not that he couldn't have. Adaptive hand controls had existed for decades. But he and David started going on tour as teenagers and it just didn't make sense with the timing. One of these days he really needed to get a license and a car. It was a huge pain to depend on his friends and an inconsistent mobility van service.

Dylan was deposited at his house first. He rolled off the lift onto the pavement of his driveway and headed alone to the dark one-story house with trees looming over it.

In some ways it was lonely but in some ways it was a relief to return to this quiet space. Especially after the grueling tour schedule of the last few years. He unlocked the door and it swung easily in. Everything in this house was designed exactly for Dylan, his size, his abilities. It was the only place in the world where he could just be. The only place he wasn't disabled by the environment around him. No one else understood what that was like, not even David.

Even though it was late, he had no plans in the morning, so he went through his night routine and then moved onto the sofa in his living room, spread a blanket over himself, and started a movie.

Yet his mind couldn't focus. Superheroes blew things up on the TV while Dylan thought about Stephanie's smile and the brightness it brought to her entire face. He wanted to be the one to bring that smile to her face again.

And that's when he thought of something. He pushed himself up on the sofa and pulled his phone out of the pouch that was strapped to his wheelchair behind where his legs went.

She had revealed something about herself that he could use to make her smile again. And maybe it was just torturing himself, but at this moment Dylan didn't care, he just wanted to make her happy.

After securing his plan, Dylan lay back down on the sofa and went to sleep at last.

By the time he woke up the sun was hitting his face through the windows. It was incredibly peaceful alone in his quiet home instead of out on the road, in hotel rooms packed with guys. He could definitely get used to waking up to peace and quiet.

5

— • —

S tephanie stifled a yawn as she answered the phone the next day at work. "Thank you for calling. This is Stephanie, how may I serve you?" It was her customer service voice, the one Bolan called her "white girl voice." That racist bastard would die of shock if he knew both Stephanie's parents were college professors.

"Wow, so professional."

"Can I help you, sir?"

"I hope so."

Stephanie rolled her eyes but managed to keep from groaning outloud. Why did white people always say that? It wasn't cute. "Excuse me?"

"It's Dylan. Dylan Sinclair. From last night."

"Oh," Stephanie said. Her seat creaked as she suddenly sat up straighter. There was a pause and she said, "What can I do for you?"

"You know that angsty white boy concert tonight?"

Stephanie hid a smile behind her hand. "I do," she said.

"Would you like to go?"

"Dylan, that concert sold out six months ago." Stephanie had tried to get a ticket but she was at work and the tickets were gone by the time she got to unrestricted Internet. She probably should have asked her brother to try to get them but she always felt embarrassed to ask for his help and her best friend Lisa had also been at work. Actually Chance probably could have done it. But too late now.

"Hey, there are some perks to having a famous brother," Dylan said. "I have two tickets. Meet me at the entrance tonight at 5:00."

"I have work until 5:30."

"Okay after that then."

"Okay," Stephanie said as though this wasn't a huge deal. "Hey let me give you my number so you don't have to pull this stunt again." He must have searched the whole company website. The directory was not that easy to find and she was sure she hadn't told him her last name.

When they hung up Stephanie felt a thrill go through her body. Her energy surged as she felt that good tingle of something to look forward to. Her audience was going to be so impressed. And she had to admit, she wanted to be near Dylan again. There was something inexplicable about him and the way she felt when she was around him.

Today Stephanie had lunch plans so she signed off her computer and power walked to the exit at noon on the dot.

Stephanie's friends were starting to feel distant. They were getting married, promoted, and moving to the suburbs. She was still going out to music venues almost every night. It was painful to realize they had little in common anymore. She had new friends in the music scene but still...she missed the girls she had grown up with. Only Lisa fought past those differences and made it a priority to keep up with Stephanie's life. Lisa came into the city every other week for their movie nights with Chance, and she was the kind of friend who didn't care if you called at two in the morning to talk through a problem. Every so often, like today, they got lunch just the two of them, no Chance.

They sat outside at a wrought iron table next to the sidewalk. The heavy iron chair scraped the ground as Stephanie scooted closer to the table. A pleasant breeze ruffled the umbrella above the table.

"What's new at work?" Stephanie asked once they were both settled.

"Nothing," Lisa sighed, twisting a lemon into her water. "Literally. I'm going out of my mind. They better train me for the new software soon. I need something new to tackle."

Stephanie could relate to job boredom and stagnation. She watched as a fly lazily circled nearby and landed on the top of the gate next to them until it was startled by someone walking their dog by. Seeing the dog, Stephanie asked Lisa about Tiny. The Jack Russell terrier was the source of endless stories.

"I thought we could both use more exercise but Tiny does not agree. I tried to walk him around the block but he did his business and pulled me right back to the house so he could lie on the couch. How about you? Quit your job yet?"

"I wish. I honestly think I might be on the verge of a story that could propel me to the next level with YouTube."

"Nice!" Lisa was the only one who never referred to her YouTube channel as a hobby or her creative outlet. She knew how serious Stephanie was about it as a career.

"Can I ask what the story is?"

"Do you know David Sinclair?" Stephanie picked at her salad, selecting the perfect blend of cherry tomato, lettuce, cucumber, and crouton.

"Name rings a bell. Is he a ball player?"

Stephanie snorted a laugh. "Are you serious?" she said.

"No, I'm not serious! Jeez, Stephanie, give me some credit. Of course I know who David Sinclair is."

"Sorry," Stephanie said. "It's hard to know what things are just part of my industry and what things everyone knows. Anyway, I've been getting kind of close with his brother."

"Close?" Lisa seized on the word. "What do you mean by close?"

What did she mean by close? Even Stephanie wasn't sure. She couldn't put her finger on the way she felt around Dylan. But she said, "Just I think he might be able to help me get David onto my channel and that would be huge."

"Wow, Stephanie, that would be amazing. I hope it works! Keep me in the loop."

"Of course."

After lunch Stephanie looked through the latest calls for proposals in the company database to see if she wanted to try again to make her mark in this industry and get a project of her own to oversee. Everything in her gut was saying no but if she wasn't even going to try, how long could she stand to do the most boring bits, the data entry, formatting other people's RFPs, making sure emails got to the right people? That was just as bad.

A little half-hearted work and she spent the rest of the afternoon planning an upload schedule for her channel. But she kept her eye on the clock and the moment she could, she bolted for the exit.

She rushed home, taking the stairs up to the second floor two at a time. She ducked around a neighbor carrying trash to the chute and burst into her apartment. She pulled t-shirts from her drawer, rejecting each as soon as she touched it. Finally she decided on a yellow tank and capri jeans. She wrapped a gold and blue scarf around her head, her curls bursting out the top. Most importantly she grabbed her camera bag before running back out the door.

On the way to the car she pulled out her phone and recorded a teaser, "You guys are not going to believe where I'm going tonight. I couldn't get tickets for the Back To The 90s tour but I caught a break today. Can you believe someone invited me to go? Can't wait to report back!" She tossed the phone to the passenger seat and let it upload to her shorts as she drove into the traffic heading for the city. Probably all going to the same concert.

6

— • —

Dylan rolled out to the living room after hanging up with Stephanie, thinking that might be the strangest way to get a girl's number and found his brother sprawled on the couch.

"Why do I bother having my own place at all?"

"Cause you're loaded," David answered without pause. "So do you want to come down to the studio with me tonight or what?" He popped a pretzel in his mouth from a bowl he had grabbed off Dylan's counter and crunched it loudly.

"I can't tonight. I'm going out."

"Going out? What are you talking about?"

"Nothing," Dylan insisted, moving past him to the kitchen for a glass of water. "I'm just going out."

David fixed him with a look for several seconds and then a grin spread across his face. "Do you have a date?"

Before Dylan could even answer David was cackling. "No way. You totally do. You're going on a date. Oh my God look at you blushing. Who is it?" David leaned across the couch way too close to Dylan's face.

"None of your business," Dylan said.

David crunched another pretzel thoughtfully. "Wait," he said, "It's that Black chick from the other night, isn't it? Holy shit, Dylan. I didn't know you had it in you, man."

"Would you shut up?"

"Oh my God, you have to tell me all about it. I want gory details. Where are you taking her?"

Dylan fixed David with a stare but it did nothing to curb David's expectant look. Dylan knew David wasn't going to shut up until he had gotten all his questions answered.

"We're going to the Back to the 90s tour at the Garden."

"Nice. Very classy. Don't make it all about you, though. Woo the girl, little bro."

"I know what I'm doing," Dylan huffed.

David fell back on the couch laughing. "You do. Yeah okay sure. You want his thing to go well you take my advice"

"I've got it, thanks."

"You should put some gel in your hair. Give it some structure. You're not wearing those ridiculous jeans are you?"

"Do you know how much you sound like a girl right now? Go on, get out of here, I'm going to get ready."

Even though there were still hours to go, he knew once he requested a mobility van it could take a very long time to actually get him where he wanted to go. You had to build in several extra hours and even then it wasn't always enough. (Why not Uber? Last time Dylan tried that the dude drove away the moment he saw the wheelchair and left him stranded).

After he practically shoved David out the door he looked down at his lap and wondered about the jeans. It wasn't like they hadn't bickered before about how out of style he was with the baggy jeans. Dylan liked how they looked and they were a lot easier to put on and take off without being able to move his legs or hips. Plus they camouflaged how unnaturally thin those legs were.

Usually he didn't care whether he looked fashionable but tonight he was going to have a gorgeous woman looking at him. Actually looking at him. Actually seeing him. Damn David giving him something new to worry about. She was going to like him or not, whether his jeans were baggy or skinny was unlikely to swing the balance.

This wasn't even a date. He had offered to take her to a show she desperately wanted to see. That's why she was going. It was stupid to hope that she might see past his disability and like him in that way.

She was gorgeous. Tall and lean with skin the color of cinnamon and curls that sprung from her head with total confidence forming a halo around her face. Coolness oozed from her. She was the kind of woman who could take her pick of any man and he'd feel like he'd won the lottery.

Dylan rolled back to his bedroom and began the laborious process of changing his jeans into ones that were slightly less baggy and a darker wash.

Then he sat outside waiting for the van and tried not to let his nerves get the best of him. This is going to be fun, he insisted to his brain, even as he swallowed back bile that was rising in his throat. What was he afraid of? They had already hung out one-on-one and it had been an easy and comfortable conversation. He had actually been surprised how much they had in common just from other people's prejudices and assumptions about them. He wouldn't have guessed racism and ableism could be so similar.

By 5:00 Dylan was at the venue and sitting just outside the gate. The garden was an outdoor venue with a main field in front of the stage and then some slightly hilly areas behind that. There was a tall chain fence around the whole thing and two ticket-taking gates. It was always interesting to note how different things were when he was alone versus with David. Right now he could sit here mostly ignored. People caught sight of him and quickly looked away. It was nothing like the frenzy of being out with his brother.

A cool breeze teased across his arms and then Stephanie was there, walking rapidly towards him looking like the sun. He couldn't help smiling when he saw her. He pushed forward, bumping over the muddy terrain, his knees bumping against each other.

"You came," he said.

"This is going to be awesome!" Stephanie said. "Can I give you credit?" She held up her camera bag.

Dylan shook his head. "I don't like being on camera," he said, an easy lie that he was used to telling. A shadow passed over her face and for a moment he thought she was going to argue with him about it.

Instead she shrugged and said, "All right, your loss." She pulled the camera out and turned it on herself. She greeted her audience, showing the gates and talking about what they were about to hear. "Thanks to a special benefactor I got into this sold-out show!"

They waited in a line moving slowly forward. They were getting a lot of looks. Dylan was used to stares but sitting next to the only person of color within view at an alt rock concert was definitely adding to it. Neither of them said anything about it. He had to imagine she was just as used to the looks as he was, being in so many white-majority spaces.

Past the gate they stopped for snacks and drinks. Stephanie carried cups of beer in her hands and tucked bottles of water under her arms. Dylan precariously balanced plates on his lap as they made their way to an empty patch of grass. A security guard passed by and he and Stephanie gave each other a quick nod of acknowledgement, Dylan assumed it was a subconscious reflex as the only two Black people there.

Stephanie spread out a wide tapestry picnic blanket that she pulled from a yellow canvas backpack. She sat and took her plate, passing a cup of beer back to Dylan.

For a few minutes she filmed the stage as the first act got set up. It was quite a line-up that included Pearl Jam and Wheezer. People filled in all the gaps as the music began.

It was hard not to sing along. Many people didn't hold back but Dylan didn't sing. He just smiled at Stephanie. She grinned back at him. "I don't know if I can trust a guy who doesn't sing along," she teased.

Dylan chuckled. "You don't want to hear me sing, trust me."

That was a lie. He didn't want her to hear him sing. There was a difference. Two lies in the space of thirty minutes, maybe hanging out with her was going to be harder than he thought and not just because he was nursing a crush on her.

"I'm not that comfortable with my voice either," she said. "There's a reason I report on music instead of creating it."

She stood up and held her camera above her head to capture a few moments. Dylan looked at the strip of smooth skin exposed as she lifted her arms up. Her bellybutton peeked out from under the yellow tank top. He couldn't see the performers anyway with everyone else standing up so he listened while looking at Stephanie. It was the perfect time to slowly drink in every detail of her beauty since she was completely focused on the show.

After a while a lesser known act took the stage and people relaxed more. Stephanie sat back down, then stretched out and lay down on the blanket. For a few moments she closed her eyes, clearly savoring the music.

The fading sun caught in her curls and when she turned to smile at him it was like slow motion. The music boomed around them. Scattered people sat and sprawled on the lawn. It was like being in another world.

Dylan realized his back was sore from sitting too long and it would be nice to stretch out. "May I join you?" he asked, nodding to the ground.

She smiled. "Of course. Do you need help?"

"No, I got it." He used his hands to push to the very front edge of his chair and leaned over his knees to touch the ground. He shifted forward until he could swing his body onto the blanket. He straightened out his legs and lay on the grassy hill, his feet falling out to each side. Stephanie was right beside him. She smelled like lilac and honeysuckle.

Her finger brushed against his arm and every instinct in his body screamed to turn in and kiss her. He imagined the soft fullness of her lips, the gentle pressure sparking desire through his body. Would her lips instantly engage, deepening the kiss? Would he tangle his fingers into her soft curls? Would she taste like thick, dark honey?

He was tingling with anticipation, so very close to grazing her cheek with his hand and guiding her mouth to his. But he forced himself to ignore it. Why was he torturing himself like this? He shouldn't be inviting her to things but no matter how hard it was to be near her and not kiss her he would still rather endure the pain and see her happy.

She was the most beautiful woman he had ever seen and she was here with him. Dylan was used to being close to beautiful women...and being ignored while they fawned over David. Stephanie was the first one who had seen him.

And maybe that was just her being clever and knowing she'd be more likely to get the scoop on David from the overshadowed little brother. But right here in this moment he didn't care.

The music washed over him and every molecule of his body buzzed with joy. The sun had set and now the only light was from the stage and some street lamps. Dylan shivered as the temperature rapidly dropped.

The headliners were up and around them people stood back up, clapping and cheering and singing along. Stephanie scrambled quickly back to her feet and he watched as she joined in. She was radiating joy. She clearly loved music as much as he did. Did she feel it in her soul too? Did the perfect combination of chords and vocals lift her spirit straight to heaven? Was music a spiritual experience for her like it was for him? It looked that way from watching her face.

And then suddenly, the concert was over. Within minutes the otherworldly feeling faded, leaking away into the ground.

People moved towards the exit. Cups and plates littered the ground around them. Stephanie sat back down, circling her knees with her arms.

Dylan shifted until he could get his arms in position to push himself up to sitting. May as well wait for the crowds to dissipate rather than risk getting crushed.

"Was it everything you hoped?" he asked.

"And more," Stephanie said but she wasn't looking at him, she was watching the people clearing the stage.

Dylan reached for his wheelchair. Now Stephanie turned to watch as he tested the brakes, then grabbed the seat and heaved his body up. He felt heat rising in his cheeks. He wasn't used to being watched while he got in and out of his chair. What was she thinking? Was she horrified? Disgusted? Pitying?

He swung his butt around into the seat of the chair and used his hands to readjust his body and pull his feet into place. He couldn't read her expression but he didn't think she looked bothered.

"Are you going to David's concert on Saturday?" Dylan asked to take some attention off himself.

Stephanie nodded.

"Where are your seats?"

"Oh they're awful," she said. "I was super last minute." She packed up her picnic blanket and delivered their plates to the trash.

"Let me get you an upgrade," Dylan said as they began to make their way to the exit. "I won't be able to be there with you but I can at least get you a good spot."

"Wait, why can't you be there? It's accessible, isn't it?"

"Oh yeah," he said. "It's not that. David just needs me for stuff back-stage."

Stephanie raised an eyebrow.

"What? I'm useful. Sometimes." He grinned at her and then deftly dodged a mud puddle. His knees bounced from the jolt. She looked away.

"Do you like David's music?" he asked.

"Yeah," Stephanie said. "I do. I'm only just discovering it really. Beyond the tracks overplayed on the radio. What about you? Is your brother's music your taste?"

"Yeah," Dylan said, "I'm very fond of it. Good thing since I tour with him."

"Why is that?"

Dylan looked up at her a moment. "Not everyone gets our relationship. We're very close. We've always really just had each other to rely on."

For a moment she looked like she was going to ask more questions but she didn't and Dylan was relieved. He didn't really want to dig into his whole sad family history. A quick snippet of memory came unbidden and for a moment in his mind he saw his mother on the phone, begging for an extension on the electric bill. Her eyes were sunken and vacant. Dylan blinked away the memory. Things were different now and they were never going back to those days.

Dylan and Stephanie parted in the parking lot. Dylan watched her drive away and settled in for the long wait for the mobility van, grateful at least that it was still operating this evening.

7

Saturday night and the dome was packed. Noise and light everywhere, visible even from the furthest parking lot. Stephanie jogged through the cars and joined the throng at the front. She looked at her ticket and walked towards the seat that Dylan got for her. It wasn't even in a balcony. Serious upgrade. She saw him waiting for her in the aisle and felt a now-familiar relaxation spread through her.

"Hey," she said with a smile as she walked up. He grinned back. "I thought you couldn't watch with me."

"I can't, but I wanted to make sure you found your seat okay," he said.

People were pushing around them, giving irritated looks at the wheelchair blocking most of the aisle. But Dylan and Stephanie ignored them. They stared at each other for a few moments before Dylan shook himself and said, "I better go. I can't wait to see the video!" Stephanie tapped the camera case at her side as a promise to create something good.

She watched as he fought to turn his chair around and headed for the side door. Stephanie made her way to her seat and for the first time wondered how people in wheelchairs went to concerts. Dylan couldn't exactly squeeze his way past a bunch of people in the row and he was a fire hazard in the aisle. There were so many things she hadn't considered before she met him.

She got her camera out to get some establishing shots. She watched the crowd and allowed the excitement of the moment to wash over her. It wasn't long before the lights centered on the stage and flashes went up along the edge.

It was a spectacular show. The lighting team played with shadows and smoke to hearken back to David's original videos. The outrageous flirty personality faded away and real emotion actually poured out of David. It was hard to reconcile this person on stage with the one she had met.

After the show she wondered if she should look for Dylan. But there was no message from him on her phone and she needed to get her video edited and up as quickly as possible. In this game speed counted. Being the first to have a piece on the concert would make a difference.

In the crush of traffic home she planned out the video so when she got home she had a vision on how she wanted to piece it together.

Despite her eyes feeling crusted all around she edited the whole video and uploaded it. While it processed, she oiled and wrapped her hair and brushed her teeth. After putting the finishing touches on the video she finally collapsed into bed. She was running at an unsustainable pace. How many ends did a candle have really? Because it felt like she was burning it at five ends. And there would be no rest tomorrow, it was church and family dinner day.

No sooner did she close her eyes than her alarm was blaring from her phone. Stephanie groaned but rolled out of bed. She had a lot to do to get presentable for her mother. She reached into the closet for the one wig she kept just so her mother's hatred of natural hair didn't ruin Stephanie's healthy curls.

Sundays were long days full of family. First church then dinner at her parents' house. And there was a not-insignificant chance Marcus would be at church. Thinking of her ex for some reason brought up the feeling of sitting next to Dylan on the side of the road under the streetlamps on Tuesday night. It had probably been years since she had connected with someone so strongly and between that night and the 90s concert it was the most fun she had had in recent memory.

Those magazine articles were really doing Dylan a disservice. He was so much more than just David Sinclair's handicapped little brother.

Stephanie went to work in the bathroom. She slicked leave-in conditioner in her hair and smoothed it under a cap. She pulled on the wig of smooth black shoulder-length hair and adjusted until it looked natural.

Her hair contained, she slipped on the knee-length skirt and blouse that her mother had pre-approved. Looking in the mirror Stephanie wasn't all that pleased. It was like looking at a completely different person. She thought the skirt emphasized her butt too much but her mother had picked it out it so she didn't argue. This was the same outfit she wore every single week but she never got used to it.

At the church parking lot, Stephanie met up with her parents and brother. Her mother looked stunning as always in a red and purple Nigerian dress and matching gele around her head that emphasized her smooth, high cheekbones. Stephanie's brother Adam took after their mother but Stephanie looked much more like their father with wider features and slightly darker skin tone. Her father was the perfect accessory to show off his wife's beauty and charm. They were an impressive team.

From the door to the pews took at least twenty minutes as they greeted everyone they knew. Stephanie had known all these aunties and uncles since she was born. The sunlight glinted through the trees and shone off the jewelry, hats, and dupioni silk dresses.

And then, through the sun filtering in the leaves, she saw Marcus. Her stomach still did a little flip-flop whenever she saw him. He was undeniably handsome and the kind of tall, broad-shouldered man that girls dreamed of.

"Hi, Marcus," she said with a shy smile. In his face she saw every moment they had ever spent together. And he was pissed at her. He wasn't going to show it, no one else would guess. But he was pissed she hadn't been responding to his texts and calls. If there was one thing Marcus hated, it was being not in control of every situation. The subtle anger radiating off him was kind-of attractive, though. There was so much heat and energy there. What was it about angry men that made them seem so powerful?

He still made her nervous even with all their history. Some things would never change. But did the butterfly wings beating the inside of her stomach mean that they were supposed to be together? Was one supposed to trust these butterflies? His smile told her that he knew the effect he had on her and to his mind it was only a matter of time until she came back to him. And then he could continue to do whatever he wanted, knowing that he had the "right" woman at home. Was Stephanie going to fall for that again? Possibly.

She just wished there were more options. It didn't seem that anyone in her world was ever going to be supportive of her YouTube dreams. For some reason in that moment, Dylan's face came to her mind. Why was she thinking about Dylan like this? It made no sense. She was developing a friendship with him, nothing more. It would be insane to think of something more. And yet, his strong arms were certainly attractive. And being around him felt so comfortable. That's called friendship, she reminded herself. She couldn't have feelings for Dylan, he was in a wheelchair for goodness sakes.

Marcus held out his arm to her. "You coming in?"

He knew what he was doing. Now it would be rude if she didn't take his arm. She was aware of everyone watching them, both her family and his. They all thought the breakup was silly and she and Marcus belonged together.

But a vision of a life with Marcus stretched out before her and it looked so boring and stifling. No part of her wanted that future. She might not yet know what future she did want, but it was not that. Still, she took his arm and let him walk her into the church, listening to the whispers behind her.

After a rousing three hour church service and fellowship after, it was time to go to her parents' house for dinner.

She drove twenty minutes away from the city up to the nice suburb. The kind of place that her family stuck to stubbornly no matter how many times her brother got pulled over driving his BMW. Speaking of which, there it was in the driveway. She had definitely left before him, how did he always beat her?

She pulled her ratty old car up next to it. Most of the time she didn't notice the age of her car but next to Adam's it really looked like it was about to just collapse into a pile of dust.

She hopped up the front stairs and pushed open the door. Nessie the German Shepard was the first to greet her. Stephanie knelt down and scratched behind the dog's ears.

"Hey, Steph." Her brother leaned in to give her a one-armed hug on the way to the dining room with a plate of food. He squeezed her shoulder and headed off.

Stephanie went to the kitchen and filled her plate.

"There you are!" Her mother said as Stephanie joined everyone else at the table. This week her godmother was here too.

"Hi, Aunt Sophie, how are you?"

They all exchanged small talk while they ate.

"And how is work going?" Stephanie's mother asked her.

"Fine," Stephanie forced out. It was never really fine but what were you going to do?

"Not letting your little hobbies distract you, I hope."

It wasn't a question but Stephanie answered it anyway. "No." It stung that her family always referred to her YouTube work as her "little hobby." They didn't want to hear about it, they didn't understand it, they definitely didn't get why she devoted so much time to it.

Her mother's laser gaze moved off Stephanie and over to Adam. Her expression noticeably softened. "Adam dear, tell us what's happening in your work."

Adam eagerly began to talk about his week. Stephanie moved her green beans around her plate. Adam did investment something. He wore suits and shook a lot of hands. At least that's how Stephanie pictured it. Her brother was two years older than her and had had success written all over him from the time he was an infant. Always in the top percentile of everything, always a charming smile, always strong and healthy. His perfection was a little exhausting at times.

All the same effort had been invested in Stephanie. Her parents were professors, her mother of physics and her father of classical languages, so of course she had gone to a great school. Yet here she was doing mostly data entry in a big corporation and making videos at local clubs at night. Not really what anyone had been expecting. Or hoping.

"I hope you sit up straighter than that at work," her mother reproached.

"You want them to take notice of you, don't you?" her father said. "Stand up and stand out."

Stephanie nodded. Actually things went a lot better when they didn't take notice of her at work. Her parents still suffered with the delusion that she had upward mobility potential. There was no raise waiting for her, there was no more prestigious position she was going to grow into.

"And how are things in the romance department?" Aunt Sophie asked.

"No new developments," she said. She hadn't even been on a date since she broke up with Marcus unless the concert with Dylan counted. She smiled to herself a little remembering it. Her parents would be so shocked. But she doubted very much that they had any sense of who David Sinclair was.

"Adam," her mother said, "You didn't bring Gina."

"She's gone to South Africa on business," he said, eagerly attacking the chicken. "She'll be back next week."

"Excellent," mother practically purred.

Adam left at the same time as Stephanie and as they walked to their cars he said, "Are you sure everything's going okay?"

"Of course." Stephanie hugged her chest against the brisk night.

He looked her up and down and then shrugged and said, "Okay. Listen, you were going to get me a key to your place? So you have a backup if you need it?"

"Oh yeah." Stephanie dug in her purse and pulled out the spare key. "Thanks," she said and handed it to Adam.

"Of course," he said. He gave her another hug around one shoulder and then got in his car and Stephanie proceeded to her own. Another family dinner survived.

Before she left she sat in her car in the driveway and pulled out her phone. She texted Dylan: "I'm filming tomorrow night at Roger Dodger, want to come?"

She told herself that she just wanted to keep buttering him up until he would facilitate access to David but the truth was she wanted to see him again. Friendship, it's just friendship.

"Sure thing," he texted back. "Meet you there."

***

Stephanie and Dylan met up on the sidewalk outside the Roger Dodger the next evening. She smiled a half smile and greeted him with, "Just how many different pairs of white sneakers do you own?"

Dylan laughed. "Guys are limited in fashion collectables," he said with a good-natured shrug, though she noticed his neck turning a little pink.

They turned together towards the venue and that's when Stephanie saw four stairs up to the entrance of the Roger Dodger that she had never seen before and her jaw dropped.

"Is anywhere accessible?" She threw her arms up.

Dylan laughed. "Already noticing that, eh?" he said, "To get somewhere and be able to just go in without a fight is a rare luxury."

"It shouldn't be a luxury," Stephanie muttered, "Isn't it illegal to not be accessible?"

"Sure," Dylan said. "It's been illegal for thirty years. But who's going to make them follow the law? They all think it doesn't apply to them and they never notice any disabled people anyway so why make their shit accessible? It's too much trouble. And too much money."

"You mean someone has to actually sue."

"Yep. And then they say, 'we're just a small establishment, why are you doing this to us? How many of you people are there anyway? Is it really worth it to make changes to the whole world?'"

It wasn't that Stephanie couldn't see that perspective. There weren't that many wheelchair users, she had never even met anyone who used a wheelchair before Dylan. On the other hand, it felt actively hostile to ignore him. And maybe it was a chicken and egg problem where if more places were accessible everyone would start seeing more people with disabilities. That kind of visibility would certainly make Dylan's life easier and it wasn't like he needed any more issues than he already had.

"You were able to get into the Coco Kitty but this is more stairs," she said.

"Right. I can't just pop a wheelie over four steps. So first thing is we check if there's a back entrance."

He pushed off down the sidewalk and Stephanie scrambled to keep up. They ducked through an alley and found a ramp on the back of the building but it was blocked by a dumpster. Dylan nodded, not surprised. "Here you see they use the ramp to roll trash cans down. No way to move this without a truck. But they are probably technically in compliance. Okay back to the front."

He lifted up the front of his wheelchair and turned the whole thing on the back wheels, reversing on a dime and pushed back in the direction they had just come.

Stephanie could only follow. At the front Dylan went up to a stranger about to go in. "Excuse me," he said, but the man muttered and hurried past as though Dylan were a street beggar.

Dylan gave Stephanie a quirk of a smile but she was too stunned to respond. No one should have to go through this much trouble to get into a building.

Dylan got the attention of another stranger, "Hey man, I could use some help. Have you got a minute?"

"Sure thing!" the stranger said and eagerly came over for instructions on how to help Stephanie lift him, chair and all, through the entrance.

"Appreciate it," Dylan said and the stranger smiled.

"Glad to help," he said as he left the club and continued down the street.

Inside, Dylan and Stephanie presented IDs and moved immediately to the bar. The top of the bar was well over Dylan's head so Stephanie ordered their drinks. "That was crazy," Stephanie shouted over the music.

Dylan shrugged. "That was every day." She had to lean all the way down to hear him.

The recorded music faded out and the band took the stage. Stephanie scrambled to get her camera out and started edging towards the stage.

At first Dylan hung back but when he finished his beer he inched onto the dance floor. It was getting very crowded. More and more people pressed against him in the dim club. Stephanie held her camera up over her head, capturing footage of the band. She could see Dylan to her side. He was pushing his wheels back and forth in time with the music.

She smiled to herself. It was nice having company. When the band finished their set, Stephanie put her camera away. The DJ put on a dance track and they bopped together, laughing. Then a bigger white guy was pushing between them, twisting his body around Stephanie. She kept trying to dodge her way back to Dylan. But this guy was very determined to dance with her.

The song changed to a slow dance and he grabbed hold of her, pulling her into him with his hands on her butt. "Excuse me," she said, trying to push away. "I'm here with someone." He grunted but didn't let go.

Then Dylan was at her side. "Hey," Dylan shouted up at the mountain of a man. "She's with me!"

"This guy?" The man said. He blinked several times at Dylan in total disbelief. "Are you fucking kidding me? What is this, a prank? Where's the camera?"

Dylan kept staring daggers at him and Stephanie wrestled her way out of his grasp while he was distracted looking around for hidden cameras.

Finding no cameras, the man walked away but not before spitting the words "N____ bitch" at her. She gasped and felt the hairs on her arms stand up. Her body trembled. It's not like she hadn't been called that word before but it was always a shock. It was meant to make her feel less than human. And sometimes it worked.

But Dylan held out his hand to her and when she took it he gently guided her onto his lap. "Dylan, I'm going to crush you!"

"Shhhh don't be silly." He wrapped his arms around her and she snuggled against his short chest, nuzzling into his neck. She looked at the map of veins raised on the backs of his hands and the light fuzz of sun-bleached hairs along his arms.

He kept one arm protectively around her and used the other to gently rock them back and forth.

"Thank you," she whispered.

When the song ended the band was back on so Stephanie got up and pulled her camera out again. She weathered the energetic crowd, holding her camera above the fray, keeping one eye out for the scary guy. It was hard to focus after that experience.

And then someone accidentally bumped violently into the back of Dylan's chair and he was thrown from it, landing hard on the floor, his face hitting the ground.

"Oh my God! Dylan, are you okay?"

No one had noticed, feet were pressing up against him as he struggled to sit up. His legs were twisted around each other, his arms fighting for space to straighten himself out.

Stephanie dropped her camera where it flopped against her side by the strap. She rushed in, kneeling down and trying to fight back people's legs. "Are you okay?" she repeated.

"Yeah," he said, barely audible over the music. Stephanie used her body as a barrier to give him space to pull himself back up onto his wheelchair.

They fought their way off the dance floor, bodies crushed against them. Stephanie went first because Dylan was too low to the ground for people to see him and no one could hear anything over the music. She pushed and shouldered her way through, checking every few seconds that Dylan was right behind her. He was moving slower than usual.

They made it off the dance floor and out the front door. That's when they were confronted with those four steps again. "Just what this night needs," Stephanie muttered and kicked the railing.

"Okay listen. I'm going to bounce down and I just need you to hold onto the back of the chair to make sure I'm balanced. Yeah?"

Stephanie nodded. Dylan pulled up and balanced on his back wheels. She leaned over and took hold of the back of the wheelchair where there was a grab bar at the bottom of the seat. With her nose in his hair, she held him steady while he bounced down the four steps.

On the sidewalk Stephanie knelt down in front of him and put her hands on his knees. "I am so sorry," she said.

He shrugged. "It happens," he said. "But you can see why I get nervous in clubs." He rubbed his left wrist.

"Are you sure you're okay?"

"Don't tell me you've never been knocked into before."

"Well sure but it's different." She paused. " Isn't it?"

"I'll concede it's not as easy for me to get back up."

"I feel terrible I asked you here. Between this and that Neanderthal pawing at me..." she trailed off and shuddered.

"I think it might be time to go home," he said. "Do you have more filming to do?"

Stephanie shook her head. "No, no, that was fine. Dylan, that wrist looks like it's swelling. Why don't you come back to my place and we can put some ice on it?"

He bit his lip for a moment then said, "What's the stair situation at your apartment?"

"Damn it!" Stephanie said. She felt tears starting to tickle at the back of her eyes. Why was nothing ever simple? "Second floor," she said quietly.

"No elevator?"

"No elevator."

After a moment of consideration Dylan said, "We'll manage."

"I'm sorry," Stephanie whispered.

"It's not your fault. It is what it is." He shrugged but looked far from indifferent to the frustration.

She nodded. "Um, so do you...have a car here?"

"Oh," Dylan said. "No. I took a bus here. You have a car?"

"I do. Will you be able to get into it? I mean, I saw that van the other day and it had a lift and everything."

"Oh that," Dylan said. "Yeah, that's not necessary. I can get into a regular car."

"Even that one?" Stephanie asked, nodding at her tiny red car parked along the street.

He chuckled. "Yes, even that one."

They crossed the street together and Stephanie opened the passenger door for him, tossing a pile of old concert fliers into the back seat. She watched as he shifted his body into the car with his arms and he almost fell as his tender left wrist buckled but he was able to pull himself up with just a small grimace.

She was just wondering if she was going to be able to fit his wheelchair in the car when he pulled a wheel off and disassembled the whole thing, passing the pieces into the back seat. She stared in surprise.

"I had no idea you could do that," she said as she got in the driver's seat.

"What? Oh, breaking down the wheelchair? Yeah, that's pretty standard these days."

For a moment Stephanie sensed there was an entire world she had never noticed just in her periphery. Most white people were living in a completely different world from hers but Dylan was in yet another that she didn't even know existed until now.

She put on the radio and scanned for old 90s songs. For a little while they drove in comfortable silence just listening to the music and then Dylan said, "That dude was frightening. Does that sort of thing happen to you a lot?"

Stephanie shrugged, her eyes still on the road. "Yeah, honestly it does. It's kind of the price of existing as a Black woman in this world. It's not always that dramatic but a lot of people seem to feel entitled to me and to my body."

Dylan blew out a long breath. "That sucks," he said. "The worst I get is ignored."

Stephanie gave him a small crooked smile. "You were pretty brave in there. I didn't expect you to confront him."

"What choice did I have? I couldn't just let that go."

"I appreciate it. I'm usually alone in these situations and it's nice to feel that someone has my back."

"Even if it's a little guy who can do literally nothing to protect you?" Dylan chuckled darkly.

"Bullies are cowards, just being willing to put yourself in their way goes a super long way." She did wonder, though, what would have happened if the man hadn't backed off. You could usually be sure that no one would beat up a guy in a wheelchair but with someone like that, all bets were off.

8

S tephanie pulled into the parking garage at the back of her building. "Oh, could you let me out before you pull into the space?" Dylan said. "I can't get out of the car if there isn't enough room for my wheelchair."

"Sure." Stephanie stopped in front of a parking spot and waited while Dylan pulled the chair from the back and reassembled it next to her car. After he got out and she parked, together they went around to the front of the building, up the ramp Stephanie usually used for her bike, and into the small dingy lobby with its line of tiny silver mailboxes.

Dylan pondered the stairs. As frustrating as inaccessibility was, he knew he was lucky. He had strong arms with full function and he had practice crawling and climbing. He didn't even own a wheelchair until he was seven and needed one for school. Even then it didn't fit him and caused a lot of pain. He had crawled around at home until the music stuff started paying off. Not that he liked the idea of Stephanie seeing him crawl. Plus with his wrist throbbing it was going to be extra challenging to use his arms to pull himself up the stairs.

She was looking at him, nervous and uncertain, chewing on her bottom lip.

"Can you carry my chair up if I get out of it?" he asked.

"Sure. I think I can handle that."

Dylan wished he had gloves as he looked at the well-worn stairs. He swallowed back disgust.

But before he could reach for the step, Stephanie said, "Maybe I could give you a piggyback ride up?"

"Oh," he said, "I've never tried that before."

"Willing to give it a shot?"

"Anything to avoid touching those stairs," Dylan said with a smile.

Stephanie turned around and crouched in front of him. He wiggled forward with his hands until he could wrap his arms over her shoulders. She hoisted him up and got her arms under his legs, and stood up from her knees. "Feel secure?" she said.

"I guess so," he replied. He couldn't object to being so close to her skin, smelling her scent, her curls brushing his cheek.

"I think I'll have to make a second trip for the chair, is that okay?"

"All right," Dylan said.

They got up the stairs fine. Stephanie opened her door and brought him over to her bed. After lowering him onto the mattress they both realized that he had lost a shoe somewhere along the way and one of his feet only had a sock. "Oh no!" Stephanie said. "It must be out in the stairwell. I'll find it."

"It's okay," Dylan said. "Just focus on getting the chair."

She couldn't imagine being indifferent to possibly losing a $600 shoe but then again the wheelchair was objectively far more important and maybe even more expensive. She went back out to retrieve it and found the shoe on the way.

It was more awkward to carry the wheelchair, its two-inch thick seat cushion that kept trying to slide off, and the shoe but she managed. If they were going to do this again she would have to come up with a better way.

Once up the stairs she put the cushion back in place, laid the shoe on top of it, and pushed the chair down the hall almost doubled over. She pushed her door open with her butt and dragged the wheelchair to the bed next to Dylan. He sat on the edge, leaning against the headboard on one side. His feet didn't quite reach the ground and his one sneaker and one sock pointed down, the toes of the shoe just grazing the carpet while his other foot didn't reach at all.

He was looking down at his wrist and Stephanie noticed that a bruise was also forming on his cheek just below his eye. She went to her mini-fridge and grabbed some ice cubes and a washcloth from the bathroom.

She sat down next to him and applied the make-shift ice pack to his arm. Just like at the concert, the air between them felt charged with some kind of magnetic force drawing them together. She could almost feel electricity crackling in the air between them. It was like they were in a whole different world and none of the normal rules applied. Stephanie decided to just go with it.

"Should I kiss it to make it better?" she whispered.

The Earth stopped moving. Everything was still. He stared at her. A blush crept up his neck and tinged his ears red. She didn't say anything more but bent down to kiss his wrist, then the bruise on his face, and finally his lips.

His breath was warm and his lips firm. He wrapped his un-injured arm around her and she shifted to sit beside him on the bed. It was kind of amazing how comfortable she felt. There was just something about being around a guy who wasn't intimidating that was surprisingly relaxing. And she had to admit it was attractive how comfortable he was with himself. He knew who he was and he was at peace with it. That must be what people meant when they said confidence was attractive.

Tingles ran through her whole body. "Is this okay?" she whispered.

"More than okay," he whispered back.

She paused and looked at the wheelchair that sat in front of them, scuffs across its frame, dents in the seat cushion in the shape of his butt, and the single white sneaker laying on top.

Life was strange, always turning you in unexpected directions. A week ago Stephanie could not have predicted she would have a wheelchair sitting on her bright yellow rug. Let alone that she would be making out with its owner.

"What are you thinking about?"

She looked back to him and saw that Dylan was following her gaze to his chair.

"Nothing important," she said.

He pressed his lips together and swallowed hard. Then he said, "Just tell me the truth. No need to spare my feelings."

Stephanie's chest tightened with sadness realizing that he was waiting to be let down. "I was thinking," she said, looking straight into his eyes, "That I really like you."

His lips twitched into a smile. "I really like you too," he said.

They were awkwardly side-by-side and Stephanie realized that he couldn't easily change his position.

"Can I help you get more comfortable on the bed?"

"Just give me some space for a moment and I can get better situated."

Stephanie stood and watched as he shifted further onto the bed, his legs flopping as he moved, and his feet dragging behind.

"You can't move them at all?" she asked and her hand flew to her mouth as though it could stop her from having said it.

"My legs? No, not at all. I'm paralyzed from my chest down." He leaned back against the headboard and lifted a hand to his nipple. "Almost no feeling or movement from about here."

"I'm sorry," Stephanie said, and bit her lip.

"Hey," he said gently, "nothing to be sorry about. I'd rather you just ask if you have questions. I guess you've never been with a disabled guy before?"

She shook her head.

"Me either," he said with a wink and she rolled her eyes but smiled.

He held out his hand to her and she rejoined him, snuggling up against him on the bed. Somehow it felt like she fit into the soft unexpected curves of his body. But she was laying directly against the washcloth and melting ice was seeping onto her shirt.

"How long am I supposed to keep this on?" Dylan asked.

"I don't know," Stephanie confessed.

"Well I guess that's probably good enough," he said, peeling it off and handing it to Stephanie. She went and threw it in her bathroom sink and on her way back across the room she shrugged out of her damp shirt, revealing a silken yellow bra.

Dylan sucked in his breath and she smiled. She slid back into bed and brushed his stubbly cheek with the back of her hand.

"Oh my God," he whispered. "Is this a dream?"

"Yes," Stephanie said, "I think it might be. A weird but wonderful dream."

In the privacy of her little apartment they were free to finally explore all the unexpected feelings that had been swirling around them since that very first night on the sidewalk. Stephanie closed her eyes and focused all her attention on the sensation of his tongue exploring her, drinking her in, their breath mingling into an intoxicating elixir. Each caress of their lips sent sizzles through her veins.

He held her face in his hands, his strong fingers brushing her cheeks, and guided her lips to his again and again. The warmth she always felt around him was heating up to a boil within her core. Every nerve tingled with tension and her hips began to move against him of their own volition. She ached with every fiber of her being to be filled.

With difficulty Stephanie pulled herself back. "Hold on," she rasped. "Let me grab a condom."

He immediately tensed. "Stephanie, wait."

She paused and looked at him. He looked suddenly miserable.

"What is it?" Stephanie asked.

"I'm allergic to latex."

"No," she said, laughing. "That is not a real thing!"

He nodded. "Afraid so."

"That is the lamest excuse in the book, Dylan." The sexual tension in her body was quickly dissipating.

"It's the truth." He shrugged. He seemed to crumple in on himself and get even smaller.

"Okay," Stephanie said, "So you have different condoms?"

"Uh, not on me," Dylan cleared his throat uncomfortably.

She stared at him, her brows furrowed. "So you know that you need special condoms but you don't carry them on you when going out?"

"I..." But what could he say? Everything had been perfect, the most beautiful woman in the world in his arms, and in a single second he ruined it. He couldn't bear to tell her the reason he didn't have condoms. His body still longed to release into her, to mingle their bodies until there was no separation between them. Desire raged through him painfully.

Dylan's phone buzzed. He looked down. *Where the fuck are you? Studio now.* His brother.

He texted back: *Get someone to pick me up. Mobility van stopped running already. Hang on for the address.*

"Stephanie, I'm so sorry. I gotta go," Dylan said. "Um, what's the address here?"

Stephanie rolled off the bed while she told him. He texted it to his brother and a moment later David texted that Shawn was on his way.

Dylan felt the silent distance yawning between him and Stephanie. She wasn't looking at him now, pulling a new shirt from her closet and shrugging into it. There was no time to figure out how to confess the truth to her. Especially not when he still had to ask for her help to get downstairs before Shawn arrived.

"Do you think you could help me get back downstairs?"

"Of course," she said, her voice more guarded than he had ever heard it. "What should I do?" She wasn't making eye contact with him. Shit. He had really fucked this up and he didn't know how to fix it. He had disappointed her and he had hurt her feelings.

"I guess let's get to the top of the stairs and then reverse how we got up here?" He wiggled his way back to the edge of the bed and grabbed his shoe from the chair. He coaxed his limp foot into his shoe and transferred from bed to wheelchair. Already his wrist was feeling stronger so that was something. Thank God it wasn't broken.

Stephanie nodded and held the door open for him to wheel through. It was a tight squeeze but he could do it if he grabbed the door frame to pull himself through. His hands on the wheelchair's push rims would be too much width. Stephanie said nothing. She followed him silently down the hallway.

Say something, Dylan admonished himself. Just tell her it's not about her.

But he didn't.

He felt painfully aware of every door they passed, imagining people looking through the peephole and wondering why the little crippled guy was arguing with his caregiver. What else could anyone think?

She knelt down for him to get onto her back and he was gutted at the thought that this could be the last time he was so close to her soft skin and honey scent. This time she held him up with one hand and got the other on the wheelchair's grab bar at the bottom of the seat, managing to get everything and everyone down in one trip. He was grateful she wouldn't have to leave him sitting on the floor but he didn't trust his voice to say anything without losing the thin grip on composure he had right now.

"Well, goodnight," Stephanie said.

Dylan nodded and watched as she ascended the stairs again and faded into shadow.

***

Thankfully there was a ramp down the side of the front door to the building and Dylan rolled smoothly down it, feeling the cool metal of his rims gliding just under his palms and letting gravity carry him down to the sidewalk.

He checked his phone. Just past midnight. David must be pissed if he was working this late. And it was true Dyan had never before had a social life or much of a reason not to be working all the time.

Even at this hour occasionally a person walked past, glanced at him and looked away as quickly as they could. For the first time he wondered if he were Black, would it be different? He had to admit probably people would think he was panhandling and call the police. As he had said to Stephanie, generally the worst he got was ignored.

He was guilty of something he often accused other people of, if only in his head. It bothered him that no one cared about disability issues unless it directly impacted them. There were so many people who didn't give a crap until they themselves became disabled and suddenly they noticed the lack of accessibility that people like him had been trying to tell them about for years.

But he had been so consumed with ableism and his own issues he had given little thought to racism. Now that he was spending time with Stephanie his mind was opened to seeing it. And the shittiest thing about it was Keenan was one of his two total friends and was Black. He still hadn't paid attention to racism until a pretty girl came along.

Guilt twisted around his sternum and he wondered how much his friend had suffered silently without Dylan or David noticing. He made a silent vow to pay more attention to what Keenan dealt with.

Shawn pulled up and honked Dylan out of his thoughts. Dylan rolled forward. Shawn's car was low and it would have been easier to get into from the street but he had pulled right up to the curb. The door opened with a loud scrape along the sidewalk.

"Hey, man," Shawn said as Dylan leaned forward and gripped the car seat. He heaved his body in, bumping his head slightly.

"Hi, Shawn, thanks for coming."

Shawn shrugged. He had always been a man of very few words.

Dylan broke down his wheelchair. "Could you maybe put it in the back for me?" He was afraid if he did it he would bump the seat into Shawn's head.

Shawn slinked out of the car and slowly walked around to put the wheelchair components in his trunk.

On the way to the studio they talked a little about how the tour had gone, being on the road, and David's antics but making conversation with Shawn was a challenge and he usually seemed perfectly content to ride in silence.

The David crew was four of them who had been friends since childhood. David was always the one who made friends and he started inviting Shawn over after school when Dylan was about nine. Keenan joined in when Dylan was fourteen. They were a team, one unit against the world, and together they had beaten the odds and gotten out of the hood.

There were secrets the four of them knew that not another soul in the world knew, not even his mother.

Then the familiar old studio where they had recorded the first record-label album was in front of him. Dylan pushed up the ramp and swung through the door with Shawn just behind him. He could hear David from all the way down the hall ranting about something.

He pulled open the studio door and Shawn grabbed it behind him.

"There he is," David said, leaning back in a studio chair. "I can never find you these days."

"Forgive me for not sitting around doing nothing while I wait for your call."

"No need to be touchy. Wait, what happened to your face?"

Dylan gingerly touched under his eye where he could only guess how dark the bruise had become. "Let's just get to work," Dylan said, finding a place to park his wheelchair.

"Uh, not until you tell me what the hell is going on with you these days. Seriously, you look awful."

"Thanks. Real nice," Dylan said. But since he knew David never let go of a bone, he muttered, "I fell. It happens."

"Right." David paused for the briefest of moments and then was back to his usual self. "Well, okay, let's get some shit done."

Keenan and Shawn shot each other a look but Dylan appreciated that David wasn't too precious with him and didn't fuss or make a big deal out of disability-related mishaps. Usually Dylan too was able to take it in stride but it was harder when a beautiful woman he really liked was involved. Maybe some work would distract him from tonight's disaster.

But no such luck. He couldn't stop thinking about it. Bad enough he had fallen in front of her but then to disappoint her in bed. How could he come back from that?

"Yo, Dylan, you with us?" Keenan said.

Dylan rubbed his neck. "Yeah," he said.

"You sure? You're never this distracted," Keenan said, leaning away from the soundboard.

David suddenly looked up from his phone, a big grin on his face. "Are you still seeing that girl?"

Everyone stopped what they were doing to look at him. "Maybe," Dylan stammered. "I'm not sure."

"The fuck does that mean?" David said.

"We just left things kind of weird tonight," Dylan said. "It's no big deal. I'll focus."

"No no no, too late for that," David said. "What are you going to do to fix it?"

"I don't know," Dylan said looking from one face to the next, all of them with way more romantic experience than he. He had asked Stephanie if she had ever been with a disabled guy but he was lucky she hadn't thrown the question back at him because then he would have had to confess that not only had he never been with a Black woman, he had never been with anyone.

Keenan leaned forward, elbows on his knees. "Have you taken her out on a real proper date?"

"We went to a concert."

Keenan shook his head. "It's time for dinner. Nice intimate, romantic dinner. Where you can hear each other talk."

"Yes!" David said, nodding enthusiastically.

Even Shawn was silently nodding.

"Okay," Dylan said. "I can do that."

The mood lifted, Dylan felt relief that the next step was set. Now he was able to focus and they all got back to work.

A couple hours later he was back in Shawn's car and no sooner had they pulled out of the parking lot onto the dark street than his silent friend said, "There's more than one way to please a woman."

Dylan blinked at him but Shawn hadn't taken his eyes from the road.

"Some of 'em like the tongue even better," Shawn continued.

Dylan leaned his forehead against the cold inner pane of the car window. "Good to know," he said, willing the conversation to end.

"Try it out. Pay attention to how she responds so you know what things she likes."

"Okay."

Thankfully Shawn didn't delve into any more detail and they made the rest of the drive in silence.

When Shawn dropped him at home it was past three in the morning. Just like the old days. But they were getting older and the late nights were not as easy to do anymore.

9

— · —

L isa arrived first for movie night with Tiny in one arm and a bottle of wine in the other. Stephanie took the bottle from her and went to get glasses and popcorn. Chance was going to be late. He always was. The three of them got together every couple of weeks on Wednesdays. Mid-week was best for Chance's schedule and pretty good for Stephanie's too. She put a circle of pillows on the carpet and handed Lisa her glass.

Tiny dashed around the apartment smelling everything even though he had been here dozens of times. Was she imagining it or was the dog paying extra attention to where Dylan had been? Finally Tiny jumped up on Stephanie's bed and settled in a circle on her pillow.

"Give me the scoop," Lisa said, pulling out her phone to take notes. "What's the latest band I should be paying attention to?"

Stephanie filled her in on all the behind-the-scenes info. Lisa always joked that she had to know so she could show off on social media but the truth was, Lisa was just a good friend who liked to hear about anything Stephanie was excited about.

"How is it going with your David Sinclair project?" Lisa asked.

Stephanie sputtered her drink.

"Stephanie...? You okay?" Lisa passed her a paper napkin.

"Uh huh," Stephanie squeaked.

"What is going on? You're being very weird all of a sudden."

"You know his brother?"

"Yes. The one you were getting 'close' to."

Stephanie tugged on a single curl of her hair then let it snap back. "I kissed him."

"Oh I see. So we aren't talking about your YouTube plan anymore."

"Oh God," Stephanie covered her face with her hands. Lisa grinned and sipped her wine. "You haven't seen anyone in a long time."

"We're not dating...But I think it might be going that way. Or I did, anyway." Since she broke up with Marcus almost a year ago no one had even tempted her and now she couldn't stop thinking about exploring every inch of Dylan's body. What had come over her? It wasn't like she was a prude but she'd never felt this kind of physical desire before. Even her handsome ex, the pinnacle of male physical perfection, didn't make her feel this way and here she was feeling it for a guy who couldn't even stand up. Her brain was spinning.

"Brother of a famous singer," Lisa said. "Think he's trustworthy?"

Stephanie smiled as she thought about Dylan and how very sincere and trustworthy he was. "Yeah," she said. That was definitely a big part of what attracted her to Dylan. He was just genuinely kind and you didn't encounter that often in people.

"I haven't seen that look on your face in a very long time," Lisa noted.

Stephanie picked at the corner of the pillow she was sitting on. "There is one thing, though."

"Oh?"

"It's just he's different. Like physically really different."

"Well, David's white so I'm guessing his brother is too."

"Yes...but it's not just that."

"Okay, so what is it? Spit it out." Lisa leaned closer, an eyebrow raised.

"He's...he's in a wheelchair," Stephanie stammered.

That stopped Lisa in her tracks and her mouth hung open a moment. "Excuse me?"

"I feel really weird having feelings for him but we've really been having a good time together. And he's so nice. And easy to talk to."

Lisa looked at her a few moments and Stephanie could practically see the gears turning in her head. "Well," Lisa said at last. "I can't say I'm not surprised. But if you're happy, that's all I care about."

Stephanie sighed. "I don't know. It's confusing. And I have so many other things to be focusing on. And everything ended really weirdly the last time we saw each other."

At that moment Chance pushed open the door, taking off his sunglasses with one hand and carrying a box of party crackers in the other. Stephanie immediately stopped talking and busied herself setting up the tray table and positioning her laptop with a movie pulled up, uncomfortably aware of Lisa's eyes on her. But she definitely didn't want to talk about what was going on with Dylan when Chance was there.

They didn't tend to pay much attention to the movie. These nights were really an excuse to hang out and chat. Chance opened the box of crackers and laid it in front of them on the floor. The movie started playing. Stephanie leaned her back against her bed and Tiny sniffed at her hair.

Stephanie fell into thoughts about the last time she had seen Dylan. What had happened that night? As wrong as it might be, she was starting to feel a little indignant. How picky could someone like him be? Had she completely misread the situation? Maybe he just wanted to be friends. He had really seemed into it. Why were boys so confusing?!

"Hey, Stephanie, are you here with us?"

"Hmm?" Stephanie said, refocusing her eyes on Chance who was squinting at her suspiciously.

Lisa was giving her a knowing look but Stephanie wasn't ready to tell Chance yet that she had met someone. Especially after what happened when she had tried to take things to the next level.

Despite the feelings of hurt, Stephanie didn't want to stop seeing Dylan. There was just something about him. It may have started out trying to find out details about David, but very quickly her motivation had changed. After all, it wasn't like she was going to sleep with someone to get a better story. That might be some people but it was not her!

Dylan had surprised her with his kindness, insight, and bravery. She had never had anyone stand up for her like he had at the Roger Dodger.

Now Chance was snapping his fingers in front of her face. "You are way out of it tonight, Steph."

"Sorry, I've got a lot on my mind."

"Work got you down?"

"Ha, yeah. When is it not?" Stephanie sighed. Thinking about her stupid workplace was one way to take her mind off Dylan's mixed messages.

Out of habit she opened the YouTube studio app on her phone. It was a Pavlovian response at this point to check her stats everytime she thought about work. Her video from Chance's bar last night was doing well. There were some fans for the group that had performed and that always helped. Over the last week Dylan had been leaving comments on nearly all her videos but there were no new ones tonight and she couldn't help feeling a twinge of disappointment.

But that evening after her friends had left, her phone pinged and she looked down to see a short text from Dylan. *Can we have dinner and start fresh?*

Sure, she wrote back. They arranged a day and a restaurant. She wondered what he was going to have to say for himself.

10

— • —

"No, no, no," Dylan muttered. He sat transfixed staring at the magazine cover on display at the grocery store. *David Sinclair gets in fist fight with movie producer*. It showed separate pictures of David on one side looking drunk and half out of his mind and this movie producer on the other, an older and distinguished looking man. He pinched the bridge of his nose.

"Tell me this isn't happening," he muttered to himself. He had to get back to David immediately and find out what was going on.

He drove the grocery store scooter back to the customer service desk to swap it for his wheelchair. He had a system worked out with the woman at the desk. He always grocery shopped when she was working because he trusted her to hold onto his wheelchair while he used the scooter so he would have a basket to put things in. He had tried once just balancing a grocery store basket on his lap but it had fallen off and apples went rolling in all directions, which was pretty embarrassing. That's when he and Marilyn had worked out a better system.

He didn't have everything he meant to get at the store but he had to get home immediately. Marilyn rang up his purchases then brought his wheelchair out from behind the desk. He was so agitated he was twitching.

"Everything okay, Dylan?" Marilyn asked.

"Huh?" He looked up at her, unsure what she had said.

"You okay?" She was frowning.

"Oh yeah, fine. Thanks."

Once he transferred back to his wheelchair she hung the bag of groceries on the hook he had temporarily put on the back of the chair.

While he sat outside waiting for the mobility van, he scrolled his phone furiously searching for more information.

"Hey, Dylan, how's it going? You look distraught."

Dylan looked up from his phone. "Oh hey, Milt. It's just my brother being stupid again."

"Hoh boy, brothers are a pain." Milt slowly lowered himself onto the bench next to Dylan and leaned his hands on his cane.

"You're telling me," Dylan agreed.

"My brother never paid me back for fixing his roof. Bastard died twenty years ago, still never paid me."

"You can't win."

"That's the truth."

There were regulars on the mobility van and most of them were fifty years Dylan's senior but company was still nice. Especially since there were usually long waits for both pick up and drop off. The grocery store run had a regular schedule, at least.

At David's house Dylan yanked open the front door and rolled in. Much as Dylan was angry at his brother right now, he could never just dismiss David as thoughtless. David has made his own home accessible for Dylan and it was the kind of touch that no one ever expected from David.

Dylan came barrelling into the room that would have been a dining room except it had a pool table instead of a dining table, already shouting "Why were you punching a sixty year old man?"

Shawn and Keenan were playing pool but stopped short. David was pacing and drinking a rum and coke on the far side of the room.

"Hey, he came at me first," David said, holding up his hands defensively, the liquid in his glass sloshing up the side.

"Totally unprovoked, eh?"

David shrugged.

"Nothing to do with you sleeping with his wife?" Dylan spat out.

David only hesitated a moment. "That's between her and me."

"And the rest of the country, apparently."

Shawn and Keenan looked at each other but said nothing.

"Mr. Mason will be here any minute for a strategy session," David said. "We'll fix it. We always do."

That was the truth. David never had to deal with consequences.

"My date is tonight," Dylan said.

"You can reschedule."

"Seriously? You are such a prick."

"Family first. Come on, Dylan. We've always had each other's backs."

Even though it was pretty one sided these days Dylan has to admit there was a time it was one sided the other way, David defending him from teasing, David getting him to doctors appointments, David reassuring him when they didn't know where their mother was.

He quieted thinking of those days and the fear that was always in the pit of his stomach that they would somehow slide back to that life.

"Good, you're here," Mr. Mason said, striding past Dylan in the arch doorway. "Let's get started." He sank into the sofa against the wall next to sliding glass doors, his suit wrinkling in the too-deep cushions. He struggled to spread papers out on a TV tray table while sinking further into the sofa.

"What's the plan?" David asked, twitchy as ever.

Mr. Mason glanced quickly at Dylan and back to David. "I think this is the time to lean on Dylan. We've built up good will around him and we can cash in on it now."

David turned towards Dylan, eyes bloodshot and piercing.

This was the role he had always played. Shield David from consequences so his career was protected.

"Or you take responsibility for once in your life," Dylan said. "Why do I always have to rescue you?"

"Come on, Dylan, you know it benefits all of us," Keenan said.

"Right, we all have our jobs to do in this circus," Dylan muttered.

"Come off it, man," David said. "I'll give you whatever you want. A bigger cut? Whatever it is."

As though David could even give him what he really wanted.

Dylan knew there was no way he was actually going to deny David. This was just the nature of their lives.

Mr. Mason saw the resignation on Dylan's face and pressed ahead. "Okay, what we need to do is really play up the strain on you, David. Caring for your brother is exhausting and you sometimes make bad choices when you're blowing off steam. Dylan, you're going to need to be as pathetic as possible. Got it?"

"Got it," Dylan said with a big fake grin. As though he didn't have plenty of practice doing this. He pushed out to the patio to text Stephanie. With his heart in his throat he wrote *Have to reschedule. Something came up with David.*

It felt like a lifetime before her response came back. *No prob. Another time.*

He could only hope she meant it.

11

Stephanie was aware of the unfolding scandal with David. In fact she had an alarm set on her phone so she wouldn't miss the press conference. These days knowing what was going on with David was her job.

Having this complicated...thing (whatever it was) with his brother was definitely confusing things. She should probably end things with Dylan so their relationship didn't cloud the way she reported on David. And after what happened the last time they saw each other, maybe that's what he was thinking too.

One thing you could say as a woman, it wasn't often you got rejected for sex. She hadn't ever found herself in the situation of being ready to go and having the guy back out. And sure she knew his disability might complicate it a bit but they could figure it out. If he would just communicate.

Instead he had totally bolted so she had thought that was it. Then he texted to ask for a dinner date. Now she was reporting on his brother's love life. The whole thing was way out of hand already. She had always succeeded in keeping her life simple. No drama. She had the right job, the right boyfriend, the right education, the right everything. Now all she had was a mess.

Her views and other metrics were definitely growing since she had started following David on her channel. And that had been the whole reason she even met Dylan. She couldn't lose sight of her goal. Her future depended on it. No way could she keep going the way she was at her job. She was on borrowed time there at this point.

The alarm on her phone buzzed and she opened her laptop to the live coverage of the press conference.

What she saw was nothing short of bizarre. How different it was now that Stephanie knew Dylan. If she hadn't met him, hadn't spent time with him as she had, she would have believed the farce that was playing out in front of her. It was surreal to watch knowing the real Dylan.

He was paraded around the press conference. A big to-do made of getting his wheelchair up on the landing. No less than four people lifted him up to sit next to the podium. He looked down at his sneakers, saying nothing as the others talked about him over his head. Talked about what a burden he was, how stressful taking care of him was. Taking care of him? What in the world? He's not *that* disabled. Stephanie's chest tightened. It was an injustice. What possessed Dylan to allow them to use him like this?

And the bigger question for Stephanie was whether she put her real opinions about this on her channel. All the commentators on television were buying the story. As she watched reactions on her phone at the same time as the real thing on her laptop, flipping between three different channels and Twitter, she was surprised how hurtful she was finding all the comments.

A month ago she wouldn't have been any different. Every story with a wheelchair was one of struggle and inspiration. Now she felt vaguely sick to her stomach as she heard and read people gushing about David selflessly caring for Dylan.

It was hard to pinpoint exactly what was bothering her. All the comments were positive, so what was wrong? Then she realized it was how dehumanizing it all was. Dylan was a person. Just a regular person the same as anyone else. Why did his body get to become a topic of national discussion? Why was his body connected to whether David was a good person or not?

She wanted to shout down all of them. She wanted to tell them to stop talking about Dylan like he wasn't a person with thoughts and feelings just doing his best in life. And the truth was, she had the platform to do it. She could make noise and stand up for Dylan.

So what should she do? Did she stick up for a different point of view? But there had to be a reason why Dylan was letting this happen. She watched, mystified and transfixed.

It's not like she could call him, he was live on the stage right now.

Finally she settled on her own take on it. She had to get an opinion out on this before the spotlight died down, before all the views were already taken.

She pieced together clips from the press conference and then filmed herself. "Why is David Sinclair distracting us with talk about his brother? How is that truly relevant to what he did? It's nothing more than a distraction. I don't think there is any excuse for his boarish behavior."

But once it was completed she hesitated on uploading it. She decided to hold onto it until she could get in touch with Dylan. What an influence he had over her already that she was compromising her work for him. She only hoped he had a good explanation for this charade.

After the press conference was over she tried to call Dylan but he didn't answer. He didn't respond to texts either.

She was already in bed, the light off, her hair bonnet on, when her phone buzzed and lit up beside her. "Hey," she whispered sleepily into it.

"I woke you," Dylan said. "I'm sorry."

"That's okay," Stephanie said. She sat up, pulling the comforter up around her knees. A sliver of street lamp shone through her window and lit one tiny patch of the ground. "What happened today?" she said.

"You saw the press conference?"

"I did. It sounded pretty ridiculous."

Dylan was quiet for a moment. "Did you say so on your channel?"

"Not yet," she said.

"Thank you," he said.

Stephanie shifted again, the covers sliding away. "I don't understand, Dylan. Why did you let them treat you like that?"

"It's complicated. But we all benefit from keeping David's career on track."

Stephanie had heard them all say it before. A sadness washed over her. Dylan was willing to sacrifice his own pride to keep the money train going. What did that say about him? It worried her. But before she could think on it too long he said, "I'm sorry I had to postpone our date. Should we pick a new day?"

Stephanie hesitated for a moment but she was only just getting to know Dylan and she wasn't ready to let go of what was beginning to grow between them. "Okay," she said.

"My basketball team has a home game Thursday, do you want to come?"

"You play basketball?"

"Yeah, wheelchair basketball."

"What is wheelchair basketball?"

"We play basketball. From wheelchairs. Pretty straightforward."

"I had no idea you could do that." Stephanie tried to figure out how that worked but there was one easy way to find out.

Dylan was saying, "Even though we've been away on tour for two years, the team still took me back as soon as I got home. What do you think?"

"I should warn you," she teased, "As an African-American, I am very opinionated about basketball."

"I'm willing to accept your constructive criticism but I should warn you that I don't get any taller than this."

That made her burst out laughing.

In that moment she decided, she was going to forget about the awkward moment the other night and just pretend it never happened. It was some kind of fluke.

***

There wasn't much of a crowd for the game. Just a sparse sprinkling in the stands, maybe one person per player or even less. Stephanie made her way over and sat with plenty of distance between her and the next person, like everyone else was doing. She watched as Dylan joined friends on the court, suddenly surrounded by lots of wheelchair users. She wondered if he experienced that subtle sense of relief that she did when there were only Black people around her.

Dylan pulled up to an empty wheelchair that looked a little different from his. Its wheels tilted slightly in and there was a metal bar around the front of the foot plate. A month ago Stephanie would never have guessed that she would be capable of analyzing the differences between wheelchairs or know what a foot plate was. Her life had taken quite an unexpected turn.

He sure was cute, though. She smiled a little to herself watching his easy grin and tousled brown hair.

Then the game began and Stephanie watched transfixed as Dylan skated across the basketball court, gliding around other players, turning on a dime, sliding out of situations where he seemed certain to crash. He caught the ball, dribbled while still wheeling the chair, shot it easily through the hoop despite how high above him it was. She had to check that her jaw wasn't hanging open.

He was at such ease here, unlike every other place she had seen him in. Then there was a crash and a man came flying out of his chair onto the ground. Stephanie gasped and leapt up, as though there was anything she could to help. But no one else was alarmed and she looked around at the other people watching. Their expressions had not changed. Feeling foolish, Stephanie sat back down. The young man in question brushed himself off and climbed back up onto the wheelchair and the game continued.

"You're new, eh?" A white woman six feet down the bench from her said.

"Uh, yeah." Stephanie admitted.

"Which one is yours?

"You know Dylan Sinclair?"

"Sure do," she said. "I know all the boys."

"He invited me."

The woman raised a single eyebrow but said nothing.

"What about you?" Stephanie asked.

"My husband Bill is the one with the orange sticker on the back. He's not disabled or nothing, they just can never find enough people to make the team."

Stephanie blinked at her. "He doesn't use a wheelchair?"

"Nah. His cousin was on the team and wanted his help to make sure they had enough people to play games. Kid went to college last fall but they still like to keep Bill around. Don't tell anyone, it's technically against the rules."

Yeah, Stephanie would imagine so. She looked out at all the different players. She saw that they had a variety of disabilities. A couple were amputees, one had some difficulty with his hands and caught the basketball in his fists.

"What are the rules?" Stephanie asked.

The woman seemed relieved to have someone to talk to and she slid a little closer. "It's a points system. Each level of disability is given a point value and each team is allowed the same number of points. To keep it fair."

"Sure," Stephanie said. She never would have guessed. How many points was an able bodied person worth? That did seem like cheating. Although maybe not since he wouldn't be as adept at maneuvering the wheelchair as the full time wheelers were.

There were several crashes, but Dylan was never caught up in one. He could change directions, glide backwards and forwards, always a second away.

When the game was over he grinned up at her and beckoned for her to come down. She made her way through the stands down to the court.

"What did you think?" he asked. He was out of breath, his hair sticking up with sweat, and his face red. Guys paused putting on prostheses and reaching for canes to look at them.

"That was incredible," she said. "No wonder they were happy to get you back on the team."

He practically glowed with pride. "Should we get some pizza?" Dylan asked.

"That sounds great," Stephanie agreed.

"Okay, give me just a moment here." She stepped back and he pushed over to his normal chair. She noticed now that the basketball chair was too big for him. It looked quite old and banged up too when she got a closer look at it. His regular chair was far smaller and fit snugly against his hips. It must be custom. Stephanie had never before seen someone as small as Dylan as an adult so it was probably not a standard size for a wheelchair.

He grabbed his coat from the pile by the door and they headed out into the crisp air to get pizza. Stephanie actually knew the area well. This was close to her office. And all this time she had no idea that a wheelchair basketball team was practicing and having games right down the street.

Bells hanging on the glass door jangled as they entered the pizza place. The floor was slick black and white tiles and there were no steps at the entrance.

They ordered slices from the counter and brought paper plates dripping with grease over to a table by the window even though it was already dark out. Dylan put down his plate on the table and pulled a chair out of his way, adding it to the table behind them.

It was impossible to eat these big thin slices with any kind of grace. Stephanie folded it in her hands and tried not to get it all over her face.

Dylan smiled at her. "Nothing more beautiful than a woman enjoying pizza."

Stephanie laughed. "Shut up," she said.

"But let's get to the most important question," he said. "No pressure, but this could totally make or break the evening. Pineapple as a topping, yes or no?"

"No matter the consequences, I can't lie about something as important as pizza," Stephanie said. "The sweet and savory combo is one of my favorites. So yes, pineapple is awesome on pizza."

"Whew," Dylan said. "Couldn't agree more."

"Have the people who complain about it ever actually tried it?"

"Doubtful."

At that moment they were interrupted by the sound of someone banging into the door. Stephanie twisted in her chair but it was Dylan who had seen what happened. "He was staring at us and walked into the closed door," he said, rolling his eyes.

Stephanie turned back to him. "You are kidding me."

"Afraid not."

Stephanie shook her head.

"Did you ever watch Star Trek?" Dylan asked, seemingly out of nowhere.

"No..." Stephanie said slowly. "Are you secretly a giant nerd?"

"Never mind," Dylan said.

"No, tell me," Stephanie coaxed.

"I used to watch reruns with my brother. There's this one Next Gen episode where Dr. Crusher notices people vanishing and everyone around her doesn't believe those people ever existed and the universe itself keeps shrinking. At one point she examines herself and declares herself fine. So she says, 'If there's nothing wrong with me, there must be something wrong with the universe.' And that's how I feel about disability. I'm fine. There's nothing wrong with me. But everyone else and the world itself has a problem. Does that make sense?"

Stephanie nodded. "I think it does. Kind of like how people in this country act like white is the default and people of color are secondary and white people just graciously allow us to live here. That's not an inherent truth, I'm as American as the next person. That's a problem with the world, not me."

"And think how nice it would be if there wasn't something wrong with the universe. If we could just be. If having the same freedoms and rights and defaults as people in power was just a given. What would that look like?"

"Not worrying about having a name that reads as Black on a resume. Everywhere being as accessible to wheelchairs as people who are walking. No sneaky fear always hovering over you that someone could accuse you of something and everyone would believe them. Yeah. What a vision. So you don't think you'd take a cure if there were one?"

"I mean I am how I've always been. The idea of taking on a completely different body kind of feels like being told I'm supposed to sprout wings. But because of how the whole world is built to keep me out it sure would be easier. Still, if someone offered you a magic pill that would make you white, you wouldn't take it would you?"

"Hell no."

"Well there you go."

Something else in what he had said stuck out to Stephanie. "What do you mean that you are how you've always been?" She knew he had been disabled since childhood based on the magazine article but she hadn't thought about it since then. She realized she had assumed an accident of some kind.

"I was born this way. It's a birth defect called spina bifida. Did you not know that?"

Stephanie shook her head. "I never realized."

Dylan nodded. "I was born with a hole in my spine. There's a lot of variety in the condition but I have the most severe version. I've never walked, never been able-bodied for a single moment of my life. So I don't really have any context for what it's like."

A silence fell between them as Stephanie pondered that. She hadn't even realized how much she had assumed about Dylan and his disability until it all had to shift with this new information. What was it like to have no conception at all of what it felt like to walk? She couldn't imagine.

Stephanie realized that she had fallen completely silent for several minutes and her pizza had gotten cold.

Dylan was just looking at her kindly, waiting patiently for her to process what he had said. When she finally returned his gaze he said, "My place isn't far. Would you like to come back with me? I mean, if you don't have work in the morning."

"I don't," Stephanie said. Another pause and Dylan waited until she said, "That sounds nice."

"Okay," Dylan said, a smile touching his face.

On the way out the door she threw out what was left of her pizza and they walked back to where she had parked her car.

Dylan gave her directions and surprisingly quickly they were out of sight of any stores, restaurants, or commercial buildings. His driveway was almost completely hidden behind fir trees but once Stephanie turned in, a clearing opened up with a large, pristine home built with the most modern trends. Another almost identical house was visible over a short brick wall, though both were shrouded in shadow at this time of night.

She parked directly in front of the entrance and they both got out.

"Welcome to my humble abode," Dylan said, rolling ahead of her through the doorway that was flush with the walkway. It was anything but humble.

"Wow," Stephanie said. She had grown up in a nice neighborhood in one of the nicer homes. Her childhood had not been shabby but this place was on a whole other level.

"Yeah," Dylan said, "David talked me into a bit more than what I really wanted. But it is nice to have everything custom sized."

Everything in the house was dropped down lower than normal and the effect made Stephanie feel unwieldy like a giant in a hobbit's home.

Dylan demonstrated how he could roll right up to the kitchen counters, there were no cabinets underneath impeding space for his legs, and the height was just right for him to reach. It made Stephanie think for the first time how odd it must be to spend most of your life in a world that is built too big for you.

"David's place is next door," Dylan said. "And our mom stays with him and looks after both places when we're on the road."

Stephanie hoped his mom wasn't in the habit of dropping by. She was not prepared for a meet the parents situation.

"She's out of town right now," Dylan said as though reading her mind. There was something in how he said it that made Stephanie think there was more to the story but she didn't say anything.

Making their way back out to the living room, Stephanie flopped onto his huge overstuffed brown couch.

"What's your favorite song?" Dylan asked.

She looked at him. "Is this a trick question?"

He laughed. "You think I want you to pick a David Sinclair? No, really." He picked up a remote and turned on a stereo system.

"You're going to laugh at me," she said, thinking of the lyrics tattooed on her upper thigh.

He held up a hand. "I swear I won't."

She scrunched her mouth for a moment, but finally admitted, "Breakfast At Tiffany's."

"Deep Blue Something?"

She nodded. "There's something sweet about it."

"I think it's sad," Dylan said. He pressed a few buttons and the song began to play. Dylan put down the remote on a table and wheeled closer to the couch.

"It is and it isn't," Stephanie said thoughtfully. "It's the definition of bittersweet." She hummed along for a few moments with her eyes closed, her head resting against the back of the couch.

When she opened her eyes again Dylan was looking at her with a slight quirk to his mouth. She said nothing but she smiled. He pulled up closer and reached for the couch cushion, pulling himself onto the couch beside her.

"Sorry I'm all sweaty and stinky from basketball," he said.

While he straightened out his legs she inched closer to him, nuzzling her nose against his neck and breathing in his scent.

"You smell great," she whispered and her breath against his neck made him shiver. He reached over and smoothed his hand against her hair.

She smiled invitingly. A second later and they were on each other. It was impossible to say who had pressed forward first but they were quickly kissing with intensity. His fingers pushed up against her temples, teasing against her hair. She drank him in, forgetting completely all their differences. She reached around him, raking her fingers down his back.

Between kisses she whispered, "I can't believe this is happening."

"Me either," he said, the shock clear in his voice. "You're incredible."

That made Stephanie laugh and she broke away from his lips, falling against his shoulder.

"Don't laugh!" he said, but he was starting to too.

"This is so strange," she said.

He pushed against the couch and shifted his weight. "You don't feel, you know, pressured, do you?" he said.

"Of course not," she said. She pulled her legs up to her chest and wrapped her arms around them. "I didn't expect anything like this," Stephanie said. "I don't even know what's come over me. I just feel so comfortable with you."

"I feel comfortable with you too," he said.

She reached out to him again. "Life is strange," she said. "But it feels so right."

He grinned. "Yeah it does," he said. The song had ended and a playlist of 90s songs was continuing on.

"Should we move this to the bedroom?" Stephanie whispered, her body once again aching for him in a way she had never felt before.

Just like the other night, Dylan shrunk into himself. Though his body hadn't moved she could feel a distance stretching between them. "You know how I said I was allergic to condoms?"

"But this is your house. You don't even have condoms at your own place?"

She wanted to be angry with him. She wanted to take it personally. But he looked so sad that she didn't have it in her. "What is going on, Dylan?"

He took a deep breath. "This hasn't happened to me before."

"What hasn't? What are you talking about?"

He closed his eyes and pinched the bridge of his nose. The music continued on in the background, Bitter Sweet Symphony by The Verve. "I'm a virgin, okay? I've never needed a condom."

"You're what?!" Stephanie sputtered.

Dylan narrowed his eyes at her.

"I'm sorry," she said, throwing up her hands. "I didn't mean anything by it. I'm just surprised."

"Yeah? Really? You're surprised?" His voice had a hard edge to it that she had never heard him use before.

"What?"

"Look at me, Stephanie. I'm disabled, I'm in a wheelchair, my body is weird, and I've got a super successful and good looking brother. Oh and magazines are putting out that I'm mentally slow. You think anyone gives me a second glance?"

Stephanie was startled by the bitterness in his voice. He always seemed at peace with who he was. She hadn't realized that these insecurities were lurking in him. "Your self esteem sucks, you know that right?"

"Oh sorry I'm not living up to your expectation of a brave cripple ready to face any obstacle with optimism and dedication."

"Woah, that is not even close to what I said."

"I'm sorry," Dylan conceded. "I'm just embarrassed. I hate that I'm letting you down and being this vulnerable is scary as fuck."

He turned away, his eyes on the empty wheelchair beside them.

"Don't look at me like that," he whispered.

"Like what?" she said.

"I don't need you to be yet another person who feels sorry for me."

"I'm not," Stephanie insisted.

He remained quiet. She said, "If you've never done this, how do you know you have a latex allergy?"

He swallowed. "It's pretty common with my condition. It came up quickly with all the surgeries and hospital stays I had as a kid."

Stephanie felt her chest tightening. Being born was the only time Stephanie had been in the hospital. She hadn't so much as needed her tonsils out.

"I had my first surgery the day I was born," Dylan said. He shrugged. "It's just life."

Stephanie nodded. She wasn't sure what to think. But there was one thing she was sure of. "Listen," she said, looking him in the eye. "I really like you and I want to explore these feelings between us."

"I want that too," he said.

Stephanie touched his arm, feeling the raised veins of his strong hands. "I'm not going to hurt you, am I?"

Dylan smiled at last. "No. I'm not as delicate as I look."

"Good." Stephanie shifted and threw one leg over his lap, straddling him, and taking his face in her hands before pressing her lips to his.

He enveloped her in his arms and pulled her even closer until there was no space between their bodies.

In the background the stereo was now playing Goo Goo Dolls.

After a few moments of comfortable silence between them Dylan whispered into her hair, "There's still things we can do without a condom."

"Are you saying what I think you're saying?"

"Well, don't get your hopes up. I've never gone down on anyone before either. But I'd like to give it a try if you're willing."

"Sounds good to me," she said.

"Then let's take this to the bedroom."

Stephanie got off his lap and stood to the side as he moved back to his wheelchair, grabbing the outside of his knees to lift his feet into place. But then he held out his hand with a smile and guided her to his lap.

She smiled and settled into his body, her arms around his neck and her legs curled under her on his lap. Settling against his soft belly, she relished the feel of him pushing them both down the hallway. The powerful strokes as he propelled both her and himself were undeniably sexy.

He turned at the end of the hall into a bedroom. The door was wide and it was a flat transition from the hall. Everything about this house had been carefully constructed with accessibility in every detail. The bedroom itself was sparse and neutral. It didn't look lived in, which made sense given that Dylan had been traveling. While Stephanie was used to carpet in bedrooms, this one had a rich shade of polished hardwood.

Dylan stopped in front of the bed and lifted her from his lap onto the white comforter. She propped up on her elbows, her legs dangling off the edge and watched as he leaned forward and set the brakes on his wheelchair.

He was starting to look nervous and gave her a shaky smile. "Ready?"

"Very," she said, her voice coming out husky. How long had she been waiting? Her body had been longing for Dylan since shortly after they met. Before that it had been months since she and Marcus broke up. Not that he had ever pleasured her the way Dylan was suggesting. Some men seemed to think it was emasculating.

"May I?" Dylan said, bringing her back to the present with his fingers tickling the top of her jeans.

She undid the button and zipper, allowing Dylan to peel the jeans from her legs. Thankfully she had spent a little extra time in the shower this morning trimming and shaving just in case.

He sucked in a breath in awe and she smiled at the expression on his face. Then she dropped back, releasing her elbows, and lying flat on the bed. Dylan touched the writing on her outer thigh. "I guess you really do love that song," he murmured.

Dylan lifted her legs, one over each of his shoulders and leaned in closer.

He traced his thumbs down the inside of her thighs and her whole body shivered in anticipation. She could feel a rush of blood filling the veins around her center like a dam breaking.

As he dipped his head between her legs, her hips rose to meet his lips and at last his soft tongue connected with her aching clit. Electricity seemed to sizzle through her center. She moaned in pleasure and he responded, following her lead as he tested movements of his tongue.

The heat and tension ratcheted up and up and up until Stephanie felt that she was going to explode. Yet Dylan continued to tease, his tongue fast and then slow, pausing at times to just suck as though drawing her essence up into his body. She groaned, trying to relieve a bit of the pressure building in her.

Then at last the tension burst like a balloon and her legs twitched as the pleasure drained from her, leaking out through every fiber of her body. She sighed contentedly and smiled as Dylan sat up and grinned. He wiped his mouth on the bottom of his t-shirt.

"How was it?" he asked softly.

"Spectacular," Stephanie answered.

"Next time I'll be more prepared. Promise."

Stephanie nodded with a smile. "Good. Now, what can I do for you?"

Dylan shifted to the front of his chair and swung his body over onto the bed beside her. "Well," he said, "My upper body is very sensitive."

"Like here?" Stephanie whispered, dipping her head down to tease the bottom of his ear with her teeth.

He shuddered. "Yeah, like there," he groaned.

She continued to explore, watching his reaction as she kissed his neck and circled his nipples with her tongue. While his lower body didn't react, she could feel goose pimples rising along the skin of his arms and heard his breath turn heavier. As she pressed her lips to the spot at the bottom of his neck where it spread into his shoulder she felt his muscles tense beneath her and he let out a groan. She kept going.

"That feels amazing," he murmured.

It was when she sucked on his earlobe, gently pulling it with her teeth, that she got the biggest reaction. His fingers dug into her upper arms, gripping her tight, and his breath was ragged in her ear.

There was no natural endpoint but eventually they both sank into sleep tangled in each other's arms. Stephanie was only half aware of Dylan getting out of bed and wheeling to the bathroom some time later. Her eyes opened briefly but she fell back asleep almost instantly.

In the morning Stephanie opened her eyes as sun filtered in through the window. She blinked, forgetting for a moment where she was. Then she looked at Dylan beside her and the memory of last night's pleasure washed over her.

"Hey," she whispered, gently touching his cheek with her fingers.

He smiled first and then opened his eyes part way, the lids still heavy.

"I need to edit and upload a video so I should get back to my place," she said, "But do you want to join me at my friend's bar tonight? It's not crowded like Roger Dodger."

"At your friend's bar? Does that mean meeting your friends?"

"Yeah, it's Chance's place. I can invite Lisa too."

"That sounds great."

"Cool, I'll text you the address."

On the drive home Stephanie reflected on all the revelations of the past 24 hours. It was a lot to process. The thrill of watching Dylan dominate in wheelchair basketball, learning that he too liked pineapple on pizza, finding out that he had never been in a relationship or been intimate with someone before.

She had never considered that there were people who made it into their mid-twenties without experiencing sex and romantic relationships. Was she truly surprised that Dylan had struggled in these areas? No. She wanted to be surprised. She wanted to believe in a happy and harmonious world where everyone got what they deserved and everything worked out in the end. But she already knew that wasn't reality.

And it wasn't that she thought she was hot shit because she was giving him a chance when others had not. It was more like the universe had been pushing her towards him and whispering in her ear, "This is your person."

12

— • —

Dylan needed to be better prepared next time he saw Stephanie. Luckily he was able to get a doctor's appointment that afternoon thanks to a cancellation. Well that and a promise of a David Sinclair autograph for the receptionist.

Dylan sat in the waiting room with its primary colored walls and airplanes hanging from the ceiling. Small children scrambled all around him and parents eyed him, probably trying to figure out which kid was his. Either that or they pegged him for about twelve years old. He really should have switched primary care doctors. Going to a pediatrician in his twenties was pretty ridiculous. It was just such a hassle and Dr. Ruben knew his history.

As he watched a child bang into an old toy, Dylan remembered being in this same waiting room with David. The two of them had sat side by side, the only kids without a parent there. David always instructed him not to talk to anyone until they were in the examination room. His brother had been fiercely protective and stared down anyone who might wonder why he was the one bringing his little brother to the doctor.

Those days were long over. Dylan looked away from the old toy. While he waited, he scrolled his phone. No new David drama. But that gave him an idea of how to pass the time. He clicked over to Stephanie's YouTube channel and put in his headphones. When he wrote a comment he got a reply almost instantly from her. Pretty soon they were trading comments on her videos like it was their own personal messenger.

Finally a nurse called his name and he put the phone and headphones back in his wheelchair's pouch. A few checks on his vitals and he was left alone in a small examination room. What was he even going to say to Dr. Ruben?

The events of last night had been incredible and also confusing. Dylan might be a late bloomer in this department but it seemed like Stephanie had enjoyed herself. And even though his dick was paralyzed, he knew there were options. He had just never had a real reason to explore them. And now he was going to talk to a pediatrician about it. He was already blushing.

Maybe he should just sneak out before the doctor got here... Really the only thing keeping him in the room was his desire to make Stephanie happy and give her everything she deserved. He rolled back and forth in tight little motions on the squeaky waxed floor, letting off nervous energy.

Finally the door clicked open and Dr. Ruben entered, already talking. "How are you doing, Dylan?"

"Good. No complaints."

"Excellent." He sat on the chair across from Dylan. "It's good to see you again. Back from your trip?"

"The tour? Yeah. We're home for a while now."

"Good. Good. Any problems on the road? Any visits to other doctors I should know about?"

"Not jealous are you, doc?"

Dr. Ruben winked and then let out a big belly laugh. "Just checking the history."

"Everything was fine on the road."

"Wonderful!" Dr. Ruben glowed with pride as though it was his own work that had kept Dylan healthy while he was away. "So," the doctor continued, "what brings you to see me today?"

Dylan cleared his throat. This was going to be awkward and awful no matter how he approached it. "Well, the truth is, I've met someone. A girl."

Dr. Ruben grinned. "Mazel Tov!" he said.

"Um yeah. So I was hoping you could help me with, you know, the physical stuff?"

"Ah, the willy is not quite doing what you hoped."

Dylan's cheeks burned. "Yeah," he muttered.

"You are an excellent candidate for Viagra. Now, as you know, my patients are children so I'm not fully in touch with these issues. Let me do a little research for you. But Viagra should be the little boost you need. No need to be embarrassed."

"Thank you," Dylan said.

"If it all looks good I'll put a prescription in for you that you can pick up today."

Dylan released the breath he had been holding. He was going to be ready next time he was alone with Stephanie.

Dr. Ruben looked over the top of his glasses and frowned. "But we should schedule a time to look at that scoliosis."

Oh great, something else to be self-conscious about. Was it really noticeably worse? Dylan thought back for a moment. Yeah, sitting up straight had been impossible for a while. Why did human bodies have to be so challenging? He glanced over to the full length mirror on the back of the exam room door and saw that he was definitely tilting to the right.

Dr. Ruben slapped him on the shoulder. "Don't let it bother you," he said. "Your young lady is not worried about this."

Dylan wished he could believe that. Stephanie seemed to be okay with his body but you never knew what could put her off and be the tipping point. He hated that he had to worry about things like this just because of how he was born. His body wasn't that big a deal to him but it sure was to everyone else.

As he came out of the office he eyed the staircase and considered testing out the maneuver he had seen online where you could balance on your back wheels and bounce down the stairs. At least if he failed he'd be at a doctor's already. But no, he would wait to try something like that for when he had his brother to spot him.

The last thing he wanted was to fall flat on his face and humiliate himself. That would be even worse than getting hurt, honestly. He could picture it now, him sprawled on the ground and some nice lady coming over to help him and he'd have to admit that he was lying on the ground because he had attempted to go down a flight of stairs in a wheelchair. No thank you. He shuddered and turned to the ramp instead.

13

That evening Stephanie and Dylan met up on the sidewalk outside Chance's bar. And just like before they were at the bottom of a small staircase.

"Ah, stairs, my old nemesis," Dylan joked in his best super villain voice.

"We can get you in with two people, right?" Stephanie asked. It was only three shallow steps to the door. She remembered how a stranger had been able to help her lift Dylan into the Roger Dodger.

He nodded. "That's right."

Stephanie pulled out her phone to text Chance to meet them out front.

They could hear Chance before they saw him, "I'm busy, Steph, what is it— oh." He gave a nervous laugh. "Hey, man. You got a license for that thing?"

Dylan smirked and raised an eyebrow at Stephanie. She could only stare. People really did say that.

They both ignored his question. "We need your help," Stephanie said. "There's a bar on the back of the chair. Can you lift from there while I lift in the front?"

"Oh, yeah, yeah, okay." He rubbed his hands on his jeans as he walked around behind Dylan. Stephanie took hold of the bars beside Dylan's legs leading to the foot plate.

"Ready?" she said. He looked anything but. His knuckles were pure white gripping his seat. His whole upper body was tense. But he nodded and they lifted.

As they deposited Dylan at the entrance Chance said, "So who's this, Steph? Are we doing some charity event I don't know about?" As though Dylan wasn't right there hearing him.

Stephanie glared at him. "Chance, this is my boyfriend Dylan."

She really said it just to make Chance eat his words but the smile that lit up Dylan's face when he heard her refer to him as her boyfriend might have been the most beautiful thing she had ever seen.

Chance was, for once, at a loss for words. He sputtered for several moments looking back and forth between them. Worth it.

Stephanie and Dylan headed inside and Lisa jumped up from a table, waving wildly. They made their way over.

"Lisa, this is Dylan. Dylan, Lisa."

Lisa leaned over and threw her arms around Dylan's shoulders. "It's so great to finally meet you," she said. "Come join me." She dragged a chair away from her table, scraping it along the floor. Dylan pulled into the spot.

"I'll get us drinks," Stephanie said, kissing his cheek before walking over to the bar. She sat on a stool in front of Chance and they both looked back over to the table where Lisa was now standing in front of Dylan. He seemed to be showing her how to do the latest dance craze. It was pretty hilarious.

Stephanie smiled, warmth spreading through her as she saw her best friend and boyfriend enjoying themselves together.

"Now move your hips too. No the other way," Dylan said.

Chance leaned across the bar and said, "That is David Sinclair's little brother. Emphasis on little."

"Hey, be nice."

"What are you playing at, Stephanie?"

"Nothing," she said defensively, grabbing two beers that Chance had placed on the bar for her.

"It's a coincidence that David Sinclair's brother is in my establishment?"

"What? I met him while I was doing the video series on David and we hit it off."

"Right."

She followed his gaze and looked over to where Dylan was pulling Lisa's arms and they were both laughing. From behind Dylan's lean to his right side was more noticeable. On that side his armpit was almost touching the top of his wheel.

In a weird way she almost never noticed his physical differences anymore. What had once been so arresting that she couldn't stop staring had become just the shape of Dylan, someone she genuinely cared about. But sometimes when she saw him through other people's eyes she remembered how she had first reacted to him.

"You don't have to pretend with me, Stephanie," Chance said.

"I'm not pretending anything. I really like him."

"And will you still really like him once you have a story on his brother?"

"I don't have to listen to this from you." Stephanie took the beers and walked back to Dylan and Lisa, trying to shake the feeling Chance had left her with. This was not about David. Not anymore.

"What beer is that?" Lisa said.

"Chance's favorite IPA. Do you want one?"

"I don't usually like beer. Think he'll make me a cocktail?"

"Of course. But have you tried an IPA?"

"It's good," Dylan confirmed.

"Let me have a sip," she said and Stephanie handed her the bottle.

"Yeah, okay, not too bad," Lisa concluded. "But I'd rather a cocktail."

She walked up to the bar leaving Stephanie and Dylan alone at the table. The first band was getting set up in the stage area and they both watched in silence for a few moments.

"About the other night," Dylan said. "After the Roger Dodger." He cleared his throat and continued to watch the people setting up instruments. "I should have known the evening was going that way. It was stupid to be caught by surprise."

Stephanie looked back at him and waited for Dylan to meet her gaze. "I don't want to make assumptions about what you can do or what you have done, you know?" she said.

Dylan nodded. "Obviously I haven't had a lot of experience." He glanced around to make sure no one was nearby. "I don't want you to see me as, like, the example of what it's like for dudes with disabilities."

Stephanie smiled wryly. "It's not like I'm writing a dissertation. I don't need to know what it's like for other guys, I need to know what it's like for you."

"The stuff with David has been all-consuming for a long time. You've probably heard that we grew up dirt poor so getting financially stable was the priority for us. It's only been in the last few months that I finally feel like I can pause and take stock of where we are."

"Seems like you guys are in good shape now."

"I don't know if it will ever feel like enough." Dylan turned the beer bottle back and forth on the table, condensation sliding down to his fingers. "There's this deep hole of fear that I thought money would fill. But it hasn't yet. You just never know when circumstances can change. And maybe there's no bottom of that hole."

Stephanie hadn't fully experienced that herself but she had gone through a rude awakening leaving the comfy life with her parents to try to make it on YouTube. Still, she did have them as a safety net. She knew that at any time she could give up and go with their plan.

"Is it just the two of you?" she asked. "You never talk about your parents."

But it was at that moment Lisa rejoined them and the conversation turned to the music of the evening. She would ask about his family again another time. For now they would just enjoy their night. As they talked, Stephanie laced her fingers through Dylan's and they sat side by side holding hands.

14

Outside on the sidewalk again at the end of the evening Dylan said, "Boyfriend, huh?"

Stephanie pressed her lips together before saying sheepishly, "Hope you don't mind. I should have talked to you about it first. Chance is my friend but he drives me out of my mind sometimes."

Even though he was thrilled to have Stephanie basically claim him, the firsts were coming so fast that he felt like he was trying to keep his balance while being dragged by a 4,000 ton train. First date, first kiss, first girlfriend, and after seeing the doctor perhaps another first tonight. He couldn't lie—even to himself—it was embarrassing to be so inexperienced. What did he expect putting it off so long? For years he had managed to not really think about it and now everything was awakening again. He wished he could be the strong, dashing, confident, experienced man that Stephanie deserved but it was what it was.

Dylan took her hands in his and said, "I want to be yours and I want you to be mine. I just don't want it to be because Chance annoyed you."

Stephanie chuckled as she nodded. "Fair," she said. She paused then added, "But it is what I want. It feels right, doesn't it?"

"It does." Dylan grabbed his moment. He said, "Remember when I told you next time I would be prepared?"

A slow smile spread across Stephanie's face. "I do," she said, "so are you?"

Dylan nodded.

"Oh yes!" Stephanie said. She leaned over, taking his face in her hands, and pressed her full pillowy lips to his. He deepened the kiss, teasing the tip of his tongue at the parting of her lips, and wrapping his arms around her shoulders. Music played from an outdoor speaker nearby. As their lips separated Dylan whispered, "Let's get you home before we do it right here on the street."

Stephanie nodded eagerly. She stood and he caught her hand in his. They rushed to the car, he wheeling with one hand and holding hers with the other.

At her apartment she unlocked her door and they tumbled inside, hands all over each other.

"Um let me just freshen up," he said, breaking away from her mouth with difficulty.

"Yeah of course, the bathroom is through there." She indicated the door to the left. Just glancing at it Dylan could see that his wheelchair was not going to fit. He reached down and got a hand-sanitizing wipe out of the pouch fastened to the wheelchair behind his legs. "Actually could you just bring me a glass of water?"

"Sure."

While Stephanie was in the bathroom getting a glass of water, Dylan leaned down and got one of the pills the doctor gave him out of the pouch.

It was already in his mouth when she came back. "Thanks," he took the glass, swallowed the pill, and handed it back.

She returned it to the bathroom.

Probably Dylan should have practiced with the pills sooner. He didn't actually know what to expect from them. And he wasn't ready to tell Stephanie that he needed a boost to satisfy her.

Coming back from the bathroom, Stephanie settled right onto his lap. A moment later she was nibbling on his earlobe and caressing her fingers against the stubble on his jaw. He grasped her head with one hand, and gripped the flesh of her upper arm with the other. He let out a soft moan. Nothing had ever felt so amazing as her breath and tongue on his ear.

"I don't want to rush you," Stephanie said. "If you want to hold off on this stuff for a while that's okay."

"I'm ready," Dylan whispered. He turned them to her bed and lifted her by the upper arms, tossing her onto the sunflower bedspread. She scrambled back to make room for him to join her.

As he lowered his body next to her, he said, "We don't actually have to take our clothes off, right?"

Even though it was said in a joking tone, Stephanie responded seriously. "Dylan," she said as she gently teased his t-shirt up, "your body is perfect because it's yours."

He raised an eyebrow at her.

"It's true," she insisted. "You are the shape of you and there's no other shape you should be."

She pulled the t-shirt over his head and saw a small tattoo just over his heart. Her fingers grazed up the soft flesh of his belly, lightly passing over a coarse tangle of chest hair and traced the dark gray music note with light gray wings behind it.

"Nice tattoo," she whispered.

"Thanks," he said. With half a smile he added, "It seemed like cheating if I got it somewhere I couldn't feel."

Stephanie laughed.

She sat back up next to him and lifted her own shirt up and over her head.

"I've got insecurities about my body, too," she said. She unhooked her bra and threw it aside, then used her arm to lift up her chest and reveal inconsistent skin color across the underside of her breasts. A slightly lighter brown stripe that made him think of a tiger with its sinewy, elegant beauty.

"I think as humans we're pretty good at beating ourselves up," she continued.

He reached out and ran a finger down from her collarbone. "I'm not sure you can compare your gorgeous breasts to my fucked up body." His hand cupped one naked breast and the skin was the smoothest thing he had ever felt, soft and supple. He watched his pale fingers add more striations to her chestnut skin.

She started to answer but stopped short with a gasp of pleasure as his fingers narrowed in on her dark areola and tight nipple. He strummed the tips of his fingers across it like a guitar string. He smiled as he watched her close her eyes and bite into her full bottom lip. Gently he guided her forward until he could reach the other breast with his mouth and feel the weight of it caressing his lips. He flicked the nipple with his tongue and Stephanie arched her back, pushing her chest even closer to him.

Then she dipped her head down and whispered against his ear, her breath tickling along the lobe, "We are both wearing far too many clothes."

She pulled back slightly, resting her forehead on his. "Are you ready to try this?"

He strained his neck to see that she had been rubbing his crotch and things were looking pretty ready down there. A bulge strained against his jeans. "Yeah," he breathed. "Let's do it."

She stood up and unbuttoned her own jeans while he leaned over the side of the bed to grab a condom from his wheelchair pouch. Holding it up he said, "Lambskin."

She smiled. "Perfect," she said, stepping out of her pants and sliding her panties down her long, smooth legs. She smiled at him, standing naked in all her glory.

He started trying to work his way out of his clothes. It was even harder than usual with an erect penis in the way.

"Can I help with that?" she said.

"Please," he said, throwing down his arms in exasperation. She crawled back onto the bed and her fingers looped onto his pants, gently pulling them down, allowing his cock to spring free. He watched as she stroked his leg all the way down. He couldn't physically feel it but there was unexpected joy in seeing someone else touch his legs. Not a doctor, not his mother, not his brother: a lover's touch.

She discarded his pants and boxers with her own clothes in a heap on the floor. Dylan looked down, mesmerized by his full erect cock. He got occasional random erections but nothing like this.

Stephanie tickled her fingers down his chest, then grabbed the condom wrapper and pulled it out. She slid it onto him and the earthy smell of damp wool drifted into the air.

"I want you inside me now," Stephanie whispered. She climbed over him, her legs on either side of his body. She looked deep into his eyes as she used her hand to guide him into the dark crevice of her pussy.

He expected fireworks and trumpets. Instead, as beautiful as it was, it all felt perfectly natural. This was what human bodies were made to do.

She rocked against him and he took hold of the soft flesh of her hips, guiding and supporting. Her back was arched and her head thrown back, eyes closed. Seeing the joy on her face made him tingle with delight. She leaned forward, her breasts pressed against his chest, still moving up and down in a steady rhythm. He grabbed her ass in both hands and squeezed the taut flesh.

Dylan wondered if it was possible to pass out from pleasure. This was all so beyond anything he had ever experienced.

Stephanie's breath was coming harder and faster. She gripped him tight, her fingers digging into his shoulders. Then she shuddered through her whole body and cried out.

Dylan stared at her. "Are you okay?" he asked.

"Oh, Dylan, I'm great." She laughed, pushing curls back from her glistening forehead. Then she paused, leaning over him on her hands. "Um, can you, you know, like, orgasm?"

"Not really. Not like you're expecting."

She gently lifted herself off him and collapsed beside him on the bed. "So," she said, "what did you think?"

Dylan was lost for words. Finally he said, "You're incredible."

"You weren't too bad yourself." She smiled. "I can't believe that was your first time."

"Thank you," he said quietly.

She smacked his shoulder with the back of her hand. "Don't go acting like I'm doing you a big favor. We're in this together, yeah?"

"Yeah," he said. "It's just hard to believe." As mystifying as it was, she did seem to be into him. He couldn't pretend that he wasn't constantly aware of the possibility that she was only hanging around him for the access he could give her to David. He wondered if he would ever get past that fear. Nights like this were probably a good start.

He breathed in the scent of her hair oil, her curls tickling the side of his face.

"Have you, you know, done that a lot?" he ventured.

"Oh God, Dylan, don't make me feel like a slut."

He turned his face to her and touched her cheek. "I could never," he said. "I was just curious."

"I've been with two guys before. The first I didn't really want to do it but he pressured me into it. The second was a serious boyfriend. But it's been almost a year since I've been with anyone."

"How is that even possible? You're so beautiful."

She smiled and nuzzled closer into the crook of his arm. "I've been busy," she said. "Trying to get this new career going."

"That I can relate to," Dylan said.

After a few peaceful moments, Stephanie went to get her phone to do work and Dylan reached for a notebook. They lay together on her bed, each absorbed in their own projects but enjoying the quiet togetherness.

***

Dylan had been prepared in more ways than one, he brought his medications and everything he needed to be able to sleep over at Stephanie's apartment. In some ways it was like being a kid again, excited for a special night at a friend's house but in other ways it was so much better doing that sleepover with a lover.

"Don't laugh," Stephanie said coming out of the bathroom wearing a nightgown and a silk bonnet on her head.

"Totally not laughing," Dylan said, his lips twitching upwards. "What's the hat for?"

Stephanie climbed back onto the bed. "Keeps my hair healthy."

He slid his hand up her hip, lifting the edge of the nightgown.

"You look hot," he said.

"Not like a granny?"

"Not in any way like a granny."

They fell asleep wrapped in each other's arms, Stephanie's soft silk bonnet against Dylan's chest.

But in the middle of the night he reached for her and found nothing. He blinked open his eyes and in the dim light from a streetlamp out her window he saw her sitting at her desk with headphones on editing a video. He decided not to interrupt the flow of her work and closed his eyes again but he worried about how hard she was working and how fitting him into her life was an additional strain.

By morning she was beside him again and he said nothing about her midnight work.

15

The next morning as Dylan opened his front door after returning from Stephanie's, a voice from the dark said, "You're still seeing that girl?"

Dylan jumped and his hand flew to his chest. "Jesus Christ, David, you startled me." After a deep breath he made his way over to the living room where David was sprawled on his coach watching a basketball game on mute. There was no light except for from the glowing TV screen.

"Yes," Dylan said, " And her name is Stephanie."

"What's her angle?"

"What are you talking about?" Dylan said, even though he knew exactly what David was talking about. Dylan couldn't even bask in the joy of his first time without the doubts sliding in. And he couldn't tell himself he was being paranoid when other people also found it suspicious that Stephanie was interested in him. Why was life like this?

"She's a reporter." David sat up, leaning forward with his elbows on his knees. He was in full conspiracy-theory mode. "You think it's a coincidence she's snuggling up to you?"

Dylan decided to be deliberately obtuse. "I thought you were all for me seeing her."

"Yeah, yeah, it's great you're getting some action finally." David dismissed that with a wave of his hand. "I'm just worried about what you're sharing with her."

"You? Worry? Couldn't be."

"Just think about it." David seemed oblivious to the sarcasm. He tapped his foot in a rapid rhythm sounding like an incessant woodpecker against the wood floor. The nervous energy radiating off him was starting to agitate Dylan too. "Is she with you for you or because she's planning to get something on me?"

"And here I thought you couldn't get more self-centered." He moved to the wall to click the light switch on. Even if it was just in his head, the normal light flooding the room made it feel less like a clandestine meeting about dark conspiracies and betrayal. It was hard to feel suspicious in your own living room with the lights on.

"You know I'm right," David said.

Dylan pinched the bridge of his nose. He wasn't about to tell David he had been thinking about the same thing. He finally had the attention of a wonderful girl. Why did he have to doubt that? Why did they have to live in a world where his body meant he should be suspicious of anyone showing romantic interest in him? It wasn't fair. But it wasn't like he hadn't known life was unfair from the time he was a young child. He got that brutal awakening a lot younger than most people did.

For the first time in years he wondered what it would be like if he were the one born with the looks. Would he still be him if he hadn't been molded by the experience of disability? If he had David's easy good looks, would he take it for granted? Would he be suave and slick, letting his looks grease the wheels for him everywhere he went?

"Tell me the truth," Dylan said, looking down at his lap. "Do you think I deserve love less than you do?"

David hesitated and became still. Stiller than Dylan had seen him in a very long time. The foot on the floor stopped. The room was totally silent, though the people running on the court on the TV still registered in Dylan's peripheral vision. "Look, Dylan, it's nothing to do with deserve. Of course you deserve love. But is it going to happen?" He shrugged. "I don't know. The world is what it is."

"Right," Dylan said. The world was what it was. Some people, through no fault of their own, never got what they wanted. Some people could do all the right things, believe all the right things, and still end up lonely and beat down by life. No one was owed love in this world and it might just be Dylan's fate to go without. It was certainly a bitter pill to swallow.

"Don't stress, little bro." David perked up, back to his usual self. He stood and said, "Just remember our situation is delicate and if it gets blown, we both go down."

Dylan nodded, a tight lump in his throat.

"Cool. Good talk." David slapped Dylan's shoulder on his way out the door.

Dylan watched him go, then turned back to the TV. He didn't really care about the game, but it was better than thinking about his life. He unmuted it and then wheeled into the kitchen to grab a beer from the fridge while listening to all the commotion of the basketball game behind him. He popped the top and took a long drink before wedging it between his thighs and going back to the living room. There he put the beer on a side table and moved from his wheelchair to the couch. He spread an old blanket his grandmother had crocheted before her death over his lap and watched the action on the screen, trying to forget his life for a few minutes.

This was getting to be a habit. He might have spent more nights here than in his bed. There was something comforting about being on the couch instead of the bed. Like somehow it didn't totally count. For what? He wasn't sure. But he did know it was easier to think about things here. His mind drifted away from the game and the beer sat forgotten on the table, dripping condensation into the wood.

The success of the music was supposed to fix everything. He had really thought he would never be sad again once they had "made it." What a joke.

Maybe it wasn't "more money, more problems" but "more money, different problems." He had spent so long focusing on this one goal of getting the music successful that he never considered that might not be a mark he could check off and then chill and be happy the rest of his life. Was there any goal that could bring lasting happiness? Maybe life never worked that way.

Either way, he didn't know what came next. He didn't know what the next goal was after *make David's career successful*. But it was well past time to figure it out.

16

— • —

"Stephanie," Betsy hissed from the next cubicle. Stephanie moved aside her headset.

"What?" she whispered back.

"Did you see the memo?"

"No, what memo?" She was already clicking over to the company email system.

"It's coded but tell me they're not talking about downsizing."

Downsizing? Stephanie clicked rapidly into her email and found the memo. Her co-worker was right. A chill came over her.

"Right?" Betsy said.

Stephanie could only nod. She wanted to leave this job anyway. She had a back up. If they laid her off it would be okay. But she wasn't ready. It wasn't supposed to be like this. Panic was rising in her throat and she tried to keep it down, tried to reason with herself. She didn't even know yet if she was going to be on the chopping block.

She clicked over to her YouTube analytics. The channel was still growing, just not as fast as she would have liked. But this threat could motivate her to freshen everything up and push harder. Being in a relationship had been distracting her. But she was determined to balance it all and have everything she wanted in life.

Back at her apartment after work, Dylan was staying over again. They had realized that with her two jobs and his no job, if they wanted to see each other regularly he was going to have to go to her place most nights—stairs be damned.

Any day Stephanie didn't have work in the morning they went to his place but all the other days were hers. Their stair game was getting better too.

He showed her a video where someone bounced down an entire flight of stairs on their back wheels but he confessed that he was nowhere near ready to try a maneuver like that and the risk of injury was just too great. Some wheelers were real daredevils, Stephanie was discovering. But not her sweet, gentle Dylan.

For going up, though, they had found that with a seatbelt holding him to the chair he could use the railing to pull with one hand and push his wheel on the other side to bounce his chair up the stairs as long as Stephanie was right behind to spot him. So that was their current method.

Tonight was a quiet working evening. Stephanie had the analytics pulled up again and she was looking for trends, keywords, and topics that had done well that she could riff on. Dylan was sitting at the other end of her desk writing in a notebook. She had no idea what he did with these notebooks.

As she continued to research video ideas, one she had seen a while back came up. The boyfriend tag. Last time she came across this tag she didn't have a boyfriend. Now she did and a little personal touch on the channel would be nice.

Stephanie looked over to where Dylan was hunched over scribbling in his notebook. She let herself imagine for a moment what it would be like to do a video together introducing him as her boyfriend. There would be a cachet to dating David's brother. Then again, probably everyone would question her motives. And Dylan hated being on camera anyway. She felt a wave of affection watching him. Dark stubble was growing in along his jaw and his shaggy hair fell forward as he wrote. He looked like a bohemian poet in this moment.

Eventually he realized she was looking at him. He slammed his notebook shut and his neck turned red.

"Writing about me?" she teased.

"Maybe," he said with a faint half smile.

Even as she looked at him, her mind drifted back to that damn memo from work. She finally had a good rhythm with everything in her life and now a wrench was being thrown into it. Of course. She looked back to her screen and flicked her pen back and forth between her fingers, banging it against the desk.

"You seem...tense. Is everything okay?"

She looked up and realized Dylan had rolled over to her side. She leaned back in her computer chair. "Yeah. I just had some bad news at work today."

"What kind of news?"

"I could be losing my job."

"Oh my God."

"I mean nothing has been said yet, but I'm not ready with my channel."

"I understand." He frowned. "Listen, I don't want you to worry. I can take care of you. You know, financially."

Stephanie just shook her head. "You know I can't do that. I can't tie myself to you financially. I need to know that I can support myself. I'll figure it out."

Dylan nodded. He touched her shoulder and slowly began to massage her. The tension released from her body. She sighed happily and closed her eyes.

"I think I know a way to help you relax," he said with a twinkle in his eye.

"Yes, please!" Stephanie said. She stretched her arms over his shoulders and he lifted his lips to hers. Then she shoved back her computer chair and ran over to the bed.

Dylan chuckled and spun on his back wheels to face the bed.

They had begun to hone in on each other's pleasure spots and each time they made love, it got more spectacular. He had found the way a light touch across her hips made her tremble with desire and she had been experimenting with her lips on his neck, discovering that kisses planted at the base of his neck where it met his shoulder caused his eyes to roll back in his head. There was an ease between them and they both felt safe to test and explore to bring out the maximum pleasure in each other.

As they lay together naked, giggling, and touching, suddenly the apartment door was swinging open and a deep, rich voice said, "Steph? You home?"

Dylan whipped the covers up over his head.

"What are you doing here?" Stephanie yelled.

"Woah, what the hell is this?"

Stephanie grabbed her shirt and underpants then got out of bed. Dylan lay as still as possible, his face burning. His empty wheelchair was in full view, he knew.

"None of your business is what it is," Stephanie said.

They continued to argue as Dylan began to have the sinking realization that he had to pee. Stephanie and whoever this guy was were standing in the center of the room between him and the bathroom. But if he didn't cath soon, his bladder would explode. Literally. And he'd be heading for the emergency room. Lesser of two embarrassments. He darted a hand out to grab his pants and wiggled into them under the covers with great difficulty.

It had gotten quieter in the room. So silent that he could hear a door in the hallway closing. He lifted the edge of the bedspread and saw both Stephanie and the handsome Black man looking in his direction. He could see in Stephanie's face that she was seeing him through her friend's (boyfriend's?) eyes and realizing how messed up he looked. He swallowed hard.

Still in silence he pulled himself up and reached for his wheelchair, lifting his body over.

"Excuse me," he muttered as he pushed his chair past them. His legs dangled where they had fallen and he had no shirt on. They both silently tracked him with their eyes as he made his way across the room, the argument paused. The stranger was tall, with smooth umber skin. His head was shaved and his muscles strained against his polo shirt. His dark brown eyes bore into Dylan, who moved as quickly as he could to get away from the scrutiny.

The next humiliation arrived at the bathroom where his chair would not fit through the door. Without looking back, he shifted his body to the front of the chair, gripped the side with one hand and reached the other hand forward to touch the floor. Once his one palm was flat he shifted his weight forward until he could get a controlled tumble to the floor.

With his arms he straightened himself out then unzipped the pocket that sat behind his legs on the wheelchair to pull out a catheter. *Hope you enjoyed the show* he thought bitterly about his rival. He used his hands to pull himself further into the bathroom, the catheter bag in his teeth, and shoved the door closed.

He took a moment to close his eyes and let the embarrassment wash over him. But he had to relieve his bladder so he continued on. He snaked the tube over the toilet and inserted the catheter. When he was done, he threw it out and then looked up at the counter that was so high above him he couldn't even see the sink. With a sigh he turned to the bathtub and washed his hands under that faucet. Thankfully Stephanie's soap was on the edge of the tub closest to him. Small blessings.

When he opened the door again the man was gone and it was just Stephanie sitting on the edge of her bed looking at him sadly.

Dylan held back tears even as the thought came to him that Stephanie was not going to want to see him again. He began the climb back up onto his chair.

"Do you need help?" Stephanie asked.

"No," Dylan said.

"I'm sorry about that," Stephanie said.

Dylan didn't look at her. He stared down at his lap as he asked, "Who was that? Your boyfriend?"

"Oh my God, Dylan. Really? What kind of person do you take me for? That's my brother, Adam. General family busy-body."

Dylan raised his eyes again. "I'm sorry," he said.

Stephanie gave him a small smile then nodded her head to the bed. "Shall we pick up where we left off?"

"Really?" Dylan said.

"Don't sound so shocked. Adam can have his opinion. Doesn't matter to me."

"You still want to be with me and my messed up body?"

"What have we said about your self-esteem?"

He rolled closer, longing to bury himself in her arms. "That it never stood a chance?"

She reached out and took his hands in hers.

"You are a beautiful person, Dylan. You are the most decent man I've ever met. Your body is part of who you are and so it is beautiful."

He leaned into her and their lips met while he tried to ignore the foreboding ache in his chest.

17

S tephanie arrived late for church on purpose so she didn't have to converse but there was no avoiding Sunday family dinner and she had never been so reluctant for it. What had Adam already said to their parents? What more was he going to say to her? She opened the door as always, petted the dog the same as always, but she felt a palatable tension through the air. *You're just imagining it*, she muttered to herself. Maybe Adam would let it drop. Maybe it was all going to blow over.

The house smelled like roast chicken and mashed potatoes, her mother's signature Sunday dinner. Stephanie could hear the murmur of voices coming from the dining room, but she couldn't make out what they were saying. She went to the kitchen to get her plate and then faced the door to the dining room.

She took a deep breath and walked through. Immediately she caught Adam's eye and knew he wasn't going to let it go. There was apology in his eyes, but resolve in his face.

He hadn't said anything yet. Her parents weren't acting strangely. She slid into her seat and gave Adam a tight smile. At least her Godmother wasn't here tonight.

As soon as she was seated, Adam cleared his throat. "I'm sorry, Stephanie, but Mom and Dad need to know who you've been seeing. It's not...appropriate."

Everyone stopped moving. Her parents both looked at Adam, eyebrows raised.

"I don't understand," her mother said. "What are you saying right now?"

To his credit Adam didn't look pleased to be telling their parents this. "I'm saying Stephanie is dating a crippled little white man."

The confusion on her mother's face was heartbreaking. Stephanie covered her face with her hands.

"There's some misunderstanding," her father said. "Stephanie has a big heart. She was helping him."

"No, Dad," Stephanie mumbled into her hands, "No misunderstanding. He's my boyfriend."

"A crippled white boy? Your boyfriend?" Her mother still looked like she was trying to translate a foreign language.

Stephanie tried to think of something to say, some way to make this turn out okay. "He's nice," she finally said. "We enjoy each other's company."

"Well," her mother huffed, "I'm sure you don't need me to tell you how ridiculous that sounds."

Adam's wife was a sweet woman and she jumped in to try to rescue Stephanie. "What does he do?" she asked kindly, trying to steer the conversation in a more normal direction.

Stephanie bit her lip. This just kept getting worse. "His, uh, brother is a well known musician."

"His brother? I don't understand," Gina said, looking to Adam for help.

"He doesn't really work," Stephanie whispered.

There was dead silence for several seconds. Then her mother rallied, placing her hands on the edge of the table. "Stephanie," she said, "This has gone far enough. You don't have the luxury of taking pity on any boy who comes along. Think about how it looks for the community."

Stephanie frowned, confused by this twist. "What do you mean?"

"How do you think it looks for our men? If you are so desperate to be with a white boy you'll choose one who's deformed over all our fine young men? Are you so desperate to be dating a white man that you'll settle for him? It looks like you want absolutely anyone rather than a Black man."

"Are you serious?"

"Stephanie," her father said sternly.

Her mother continued. "This is part of the nature of racism. What you do doesn't just effect you. What you do has implications for all of us."

"That's not fair—"

"No, it's not. But that's our reality. You can't just do whatever you please without thinking about how it impacts the rest of us."

Stephanie was at a loss for words. There was no answer to that. Though she was sorely tempted to point out that plenty of Black men had no trouble refusing to give a Black woman a chance. And she had not forgotten Adam's college girlfriend, a whimpering little white girl. Now Adam had what Stephanie wished she did. His relationship with Gina was an inspiration. She had thought with Marcus she would have what they had but now she knew how rare and special that love was.

"Break it off now," her father said, "before he gets too attached to you."

Clearly it didn't occur to her parents that she might also be attached to him. You couldn't really fall for a disabled man, right?

"We'll introduce you to some of our friends!" Gina jumped in eagerly. "We know lots of eligible guys. Good looking, great jobs, ready to meet someone."

Stephanie nodded because what else could she do? She felt as though a beautiful dream she had been floating in had suddenly ended and she had to come back to reality. How could she ever be with Dylan long term? She couldn't imagine bringing him here, having him around the table just part of the family like Adam's wife was. How had she allowed herself to fall so deeply into this dream life that couldn't survive in the real world?

"I'm sorry," Adam said. "But it's for the best."

Stephanie left the dinner shaken. Most of her family's objections to Dylan didn't matter to her. Him being white, him needing a wheelchair. So what? It wasn't her job to make Black men look good.

But not having a job. That one ate at her. She was ambitious, how could she have a partner who didn't want to leave his mark on the world?

She thought back on all the time they spent together and it was all shadowed by this new thought. She hadn't noticed before. She had been too enrapt in the giddy buzz of a new relationship. But now it was a huge glaring hole. He didn't work. He didn't do anything. He just followed his brother around. While Stephanie worked a full time job on top of a side hustle.

Much as she hated herself a little for it, she couldn't quite look at him the same way.

18

—·—

Dylan had left the door unlocked for her and Stephanie was greeted by the smell of roasting chicken and garlic as she walked into his house. Before he noticed her she stood in the doorway and watched him. Dylan was sitting at the kitchen table, chopping vegetables. He was wearing a plain white T-shirt and jeans, and he had a pair of headphones on.

"Oh hey," he said when he noticed her. He slipped the headphones down around his neck and she could hear the faint melody of Semi-Charmed Life drifting from them. "Come and taste the sauce." He pushed back from the table and rolled backwards to the stove.

She shrugged out of her coat, draped it over her arm, and stepped further into the kitchen.

"What are you making?" she said, looking over his shoulder as she joined him at the low stove.

"Spaghetti," he said. He held up a spoon with a little tomato sauce on it. She bent down to eat it. He looked at her expectantly but she couldn't tell him the truth. Looking around she wasn't surprised to see the only seasonings were salt and garlic salt. It was pretty bland but she smiled and said it was good because it wasn't every day a boyfriend cooked for her. The gesture was kind and Stephanie appreciated it.

"Sit down, tell me about your day."

Stephanie sat down in the only chair at the kitchen table but she didn't have much to say. The evening with her family was still bothering her and she was afraid to bring it up. Instead she commented on the music and they talked about that instead as Dylan moved the cutting board of vegetables onto his lap and brought it over to the sauce.

Soon after the meal was done and Dylan brought over two plates of spaghetti with roast chicken on top balanced on the same cutting board. He placed one in front of her and said, "Don't get used to it, this is the only thing I know how to cook."

She tried to laugh but it died in her throat and she just managed half a smile. He looked confused by her reticence and she wished she knew how to fix waht she was feeling. As they ate it was so quiet she could hear a clock ticking somewhere in another room and the clink of her fork against the plate.

"Everything okay?" Dylan finally said. "You seem distant."

Stephanie forced herself to stop moving the chicken around on her plate and really look him in the eye. "Adam told my parents about you," she said.

"Oh." He put his fork down. His face seemed to drain of what little color it had. "Didn't go well, I take it."

She shook her head.

"Not that I'm surprised."

She sighed. "Has anyone ever told you your self esteem sucks?"

He pressed his lips together so hard they disappeared. "And where exactly do you expect me to get self esteem from? My brother who has such a large shadow no one knows I exist?"

This time Stephanie didn't back down. "Whose fault is that, though? You decided to follow him around and ride his coattails."

"I did *what* now?" He stared at her, wide-eyed with shock.

"Have you ever even tried to go out on your own? To do something that is fully yours?" The floodgates had opened and now Stephanie couldn't stop even if she wanted to. Every frustration was coming out of her, no matter how hurtful it might be.

Dylan sucked air in through his nose, clearly trying to keep his cool. "You have no idea what you're talking about."

"Don't try to tell me that you can't go out and find your own path just because you're in a wheelchair."

He slammed his hands against the table, rattling the plates. "My wheelchair has nothing to do with why I haven't made a name for myself separate from David."

"Well then why haven't you?"

"We need each other. You will never understand that," he spat out.

"Oh yeah, I've never had complicated relationships with family members."

"Not like this you haven't."

"Aren't you tired of living off your brother? Don't you want to do anything for yourself?"

His jaw tightened. She could see every muscle in his neck. He said nothing.

She pushed back from the table and leaned towards his face. "It's hard to take you seriously when you aren't even trying," she said. "I work my butt off to make a better future for myself and what are you doing?"

"It's me," he burst out. "It's me, Stephanie. All of it. It's all me and it always has been. The entire David Sinclair brand. It's me." He punctuated each sentence with a punch to his lap, shaking one foot off the footplate and onto the floor. "*I* write the music. *I* sing the songs. He looks pretty and *I* do the work! I started that YouTube Channel and I sang my heart out to save my family and I don't ever get to let anyone know that I did that. I did that single handedly. It's all because of me. We aren't digging in couch cushions for pennies because of ME."

"Wow, just when I thought you couldn't sink any lower. I can't believe you're desperate enough to impress me that you'll take credit for his work. That's really pathetic, Dylan. I think we're done here." She grabbed her coat and headed for the door. Dylan said nothing to stop her.

19

D avid burst into the house the next day, the front door banging against the wall, and startled Dylan awake from where he had fallen asleep on the couch again. He blinked groggily.

"Why are you moping around?" His brother shoved a curtain open with a violent swish that let in a swatch of sunlight directly onto Dylan's face.

He let out a low moan and instinctively reached to cover his eyes, feeling the rough stubble on his cheeks. His voice was scratchy as he mumbled, "I'm not moping, I'm just resting."

"Bullshit," David said. He plopped down beside Dylan's legs on the couch, the cushions sinking slightly under his weight, and Dylan's legs falling towards the indent.

David's piercing gaze locked onto his younger brother, and for a moment, it felt as if he could read Dylan's thoughts just by looking at him. "She broke up with you?" David asked bluntly.

Dylan hesitated for a moment, his heart sinking at the memory of the painful conversation with Stephanie. "Yeah," he admitted.

"You didn't tell her, did you?"

There was no way Dylan was going to admit to his brother that he had indeed shared their secret with someone who could very easily use it against them. It was probably a good thing that she hadn't believed him but it still stung.

"Dylan?" David prompted, waiting for an answer.

"No," he managed to reply, avoiding David's intense gaze. Struggling to sit up, Dylan's head pounded with each movement. A hazy recollection of the previous night floated through his brain. He had gotten drunk last night after Stephanie left. In fact, empty cans of beer were lined up on the floor next to the couch. David was looking at them too.

"Women are quite the experience," David said.

"Don't," Dylan said, dropping his head back down on the couch cushion to stop the pounding.

But David persisted. "What? I'm helping you through your first heartbreak. A little late in life, but better late than never." He shrugged.

"Who says it's the first?" Dylan spat out.

The atmosphere in the room shifted. David's eyes flickered with understanding. He knew exactly what Dylan meant. Even if he hadn't ever dated someone before, Dylan had experienced desire and feelings that went unrequited. Maybe if they hadn't built such a convincing mirage, more women would see value in Dylan. Instead, everything in his life was set up to call him a loser.

"She's not special, Dylan. You'll find another girl. Your cherry's been popped, it will be easier next time."

Dylan winced at the crude analogy. "Don't say that about her, she is different."

David shook his head. "She's like every other girl out there and I'll prove it to you."

Dylan stared at his brother. This couldn't be good. "What are you going to do?"

A devious smirk played on David's lips. "She wants David Sinclair, I'll give her David Sinclair. She'll fall all over herself to be with me and you'll see that this has all been about getting close to me."

It felt like a punch in the gut and Dylan struggled for a moment to catch his breath. What would Stephanie do if David started coming on to her? He didn't want to know. "Please, David, you've already taken everything from me."

David stood up and shook his head slowly. "Oh Dylan, don't twist it in your mind. I took nothing, you willingly gave everything."

There was nothing he could say to that. It was true. All of this had been his idea and now that he wanted to stop the ride, too many other people depended on the lie.

Before leaving, David turned back and said, "If I find you still on the couch when I get home I'm going to check you for bed sores myself. Don't think I won't."

Dylan nodded weakly, feeling defeated and exhausted as he watched David leave. Despite the threat, Dylan closed his eyes and went back to sleep.

20

— · —

Stephanie had not realized what a huge part of her life Dylan had become. His absence was an enormous hole. She couldn't turn on the radio without hearing his brother and feeling a rush of mixed emotions, both anger at his lies and sadness that he wasn't with her. She looked at her YouTube comments and missed their little conversations there.

Fewer and fewer assignments crossed her desk at work. The signs were clear that she wasn't going to last much longer. Time to start polishing up her resume and looking for another day job to keep her going while she toiled on the channel. She didn't have any savings to fall back on so she needed to get out ahead of the layoffs.

One week at family dinner after church she walked into the dining room and Marcus was sitting there. From the doorway she watched as he laughed and chatted with her family as though he had never left.

Her heart settled itself in resignation. This was how it should be. She slid into the chair beside him and he put a hand on her thigh under the table as he continued his conversation. She felt the cage closing in around her and the memory of their last fight came back to her. They had broken up because Marcus didn't like her going out nearly every night especially if she was out without him. If she let this relationship start up again, it would be the end of her music journalism.

She would become what everyone was waiting for her to become, a grownup with a job and no passions. Maybe it was time. Maybe she should shut herself down inside and stop trying to fight the current.

Abruptly, Stephanie burst out, "I'm sorry, I can't do this." Her plate untouched, she shoved her chair back from the table and bolted towards the stairs and her childhood bedroom with the sound of her father calling her name sharply following at her heels.

She shut the door and ran to her bed, lying back and letting the tears slip from the sides of her eyes, wetting the sides of her face, and soaking into the comforter.

Her parents should have waited longer before inviting Marcus back over. Not that they knew she and Dylan had broken up. In fact, they couldn't even process the idea that she might have cared about him, that she might be missing him. He was never mentioned.

It didn't make logical sense. She knew how it looked. How could she be mooning over a "crippled little white man with no job"? And yet.

She remembered what Lisa had said. The heart doesn't make sense. Love doesn't happen in the brain.

She would get over it eventually. People did. Her heart would heal, she would move on. She would think back wistfully about the time she dated David Sinclair's brother. But not yet.

Then there was a gentle knock on the door. Who was that? Not her father, whose knock was always sharp and forceful and not her mother who never made the first move after a fight but waited for an apology to come to her.

"Yes?" she said.

Adam peered around the door. "May I come in?"

"You knocked," Stephanie said, surprise and awe in her voice.

"I learned my lesson." He gave a small smile as he came into the room and sat down on the edge of her bed. He cleared his throat. "So I noticed you haven't posted to your channel in a couple weeks."

Stephanie shrugged. "Yeah, maybe it really is time to stop." Her gut twisted at the words. It was hard to envision any kind of happy life working in an office like the one she was in now.

"You broke up with...sorry, what was his name?"

"Dylan," Stephanie said, somehow not even surprised that Adam didn't know his name. "And yes, we broke up."

"I'm sorry," Adam said.

Stephanie shrugged sadly. "You were right," she said. "He doesn't have a job, he just coasts on what his brother does."

Adam nodded. After a moment he said, "Marcus is being very attentive today."

"Yeah," she said.

It was true and what more could you ask for? Their breakup had been dumb. You couldn't have everything so you had to compromise a bit to get a good life. A handsome husband, that her family approved of, who made a good living. What was there not to like? And unlike Dylan, Marcus had never lied to her. His only crime was that he didn't believe in her channel. And okay he was a little arrogant but everyone has flaws.

"But you're not ready to move on from Dylan yet."

Stephanie scrunched her eyes closed and tried not to cry again. Her brother could be surprisingly insightful at times.

Adam put his hand on her shoulder. "So go ahead, tell me what you like about him."

She smiled. She let her mind drift back, remembering each moment with Dylan. When had she started to really like him in that way? What had made her want to date him? She pulled her bedspread around her like a cocoon and said, "He's really kind. Not for show, kind in a completely sincere and genuine way. Thoughtful gestures come naturally to him. He listens and pays attention." She thought back to the Roger Dodger when Dylan had shouted at a man towering over him. "He defended me against an aggressive guy at a club even though he could have been seriously hurt. He's a good person. Maybe the best person I've ever met."

Adam nodded slowly. "I'm sorry I reacted the way I did," he said. "I should have trusted your judgment more."

Stephanie sighed. "It was doomed from the start. How did I ever think we would have a future together?"

"Give yourself time to grieve," Adam said. "It was important to you. He was important to you. And there's nothing wrong with that." He gave her one more pat on her shoulder and got up. "I'll smooth things over with Mom, Dad, and Marcus, okay?"

"Thank you," Stephanie said quietly. She closed her eyes and imagined her favorite songs in her mind to soothe her to sleep.

***

Stephanie wasn't particularly in the mood for her friend movie night but she also didn't want to come up with an excuse. As usual, Lisa arrived first with Tiny, who seemed to immediately know that Stephanie could use cheering up. Tiny climbed right into her lap and settled his head on her knee. Lisa got the drinks and sat down next to Stephanie on the floor.

"Is Dylan joining us tonight?" Lisa asked as she smoothed out her flowing floral skirt.

"No," Stephanie said looking down at the dog, who licked her finger and whimpered.

"What's wrong?" Lisa asked, always attuned to what Tiny was doing.

Stephanie swallowed hard and forced back tears. "I'm not seeing him any more."

"Oh no!" Lisa said. "He was so nice. Or are we angry with him...?"

"No, he is nice. He's very sweet. But what kind of a future could we have?"

"Uh....any kind you want? Stephanie, what happened?"

She looked at the time on her phone. Chance probably wouldn't be here for another few minutes. "Adam came by my place unexpectedly and saw him."

Lisa arched an eyebrow. "Saw him? Have you been hiding him?"

That was the question, wasn't it? She hadn't meant to hide him and yet she definitely had not wanted her family to know about him.

"I don't know. Kind of. Not from you, obviously. But family is tricky," she said.

"I hear that."

"How do you think your family would react if you brought home a white boy in a wheelchair?"

She quirked a smile and said, "They might be relieved I brought anyone home. The 'when are my grandbabies coming' conversations with my mom are getting intense."

Stephanie wanted to laugh but she was in too much internal turmoil. She pressed her lips together and looked down at the carpet.

Lisa observed her for a moment then said, "So Adam met Dylan and was not impressed so you broke up with him?"

"You know how horrible that sounds."

"I do."

"It's more complicated than that. Dylan doesn't work."

"Might be hard for him to find a job. I mean I'm sure he's perfectly capable of, like, computer stuff maybe. But it's going to be hard. I don't know any people in wheelchairs at my job. What about yours?"

Stephanie shook her head. And now that Lisa mentioned computers she had to wonder if Dylan had had the chance at education like she did. No, she knew he didn't have even close to the education she had. She knew he had grown up poor. Did he ever get the chance to learn skills he could do from a wheelchair? Probably not.

"Well the worst thing is that he lied when I brought it up."

"What did he say?"

Stephanie shook her head. "It's too ridiculous."

"I'm sorry, sweetie," Lisa said.

Then Chance arrived and looked back and forth between them, sensing he had missed something. He wasn't usually perceptive but he might be starting to notice that a lot tended to happen before he showed up for their movie nights. But he didn't say anything and they all settled in to watch an old movie on the laptop and gossip.

***

The last person Stephanie expected to see as she wheeled her bicycle out to the street after work was David. His disguise was the opposite of helpful, just making him stand out more for looking ridiculous. Slouchy beanie hat, sunglasses at night. But it must have been working to some degree because there were no fan girls surrounding him and no entourage either. He was alone. She had never seen him alone. Was he here to plead a case for Dylan? To ask her to reconsider?

She stopped in front of him. With his sunglasses on she couldn't see his eyes. She crossed her arms. "What are you doing here?"

He slid the sunglasses down and gave a sardonic smile. "Such a charmer," he said, "I get what Dylan sees in you."

"If you're here to convince me to get back together with him..."

David interrupted her with a barking laugh. "No, Stephanie, that's not why I'm here."

"Well?" She glared at him.

"You've gone above and beyond for your goals and I admire that. We all know what this has really been about. From day one you've wanted me to save your channel and you've been willing to do anything, even degrading yourself to do it. Well you can stop. I'm here and I'm willing to give you what you want...if you give me just a little of what I want."

Stephanie stared at him. Was she really hearing what she thought she was hearing?

"You really think you're a catch, don't you?" she said, shaking her head slowly.

He leaned closer to her. "This is what you want, Stephanie. Don't be a jerk or I'll change my mind."

Did he have a point? Was this what she had really been waiting for this whole time? Maybe it would be wise to give in to him. Maybe it was smart to take this offering. But every instinct and fiber in her body pulled against the idea. Even if she and Dylan never saw each other again. Even if she never made her channel a success. Even if she was stuck in a dead end job for the rest of her life. She could rest assured that even subconsciously a desire for David was not what motivated her to date Dylan. Dylan had been his own reward.

"You're not a catch," she said, "You're an asshole. You're not half the man your brother is." She started to push past him but he reached for her and she slapped his hand away.

"Are you fucking serious?" David said.

"Is it so hard to believe that I wanted to be with Dylan? That I liked him?"

"Frankly, yes. I mean, I love the kid but let's be real, he was dealt a shit hand in life and it's no one's fault but he's not what anyone would call desirable. Don't lie to me, you felt the same."

"Yes, I did but that's the past tense. Who he is as a person overshadows anything unattractive about his body."

"So you're really choosing him over your channel, your future, and your career?"

Her gut twisted but she didn't let it show. She wasn't going to let David know he was getting to her. "Lucky for me, you don't control the success of my future. I'm going to do it and I'm going to do it without you."

"Ha. Your funeral but I hope you're happy and don't start resenting him."

"You are a real piece of work."

David grinned and dipped his head as though tipping a hat. "Why thank you."

21

D ylan felt stuck in a loop, the same story playing out over and over again in his life and he couldn't see any way out of it. There was one person whose insight he desperately needed and so he found himself on a bus heading up into the hills towards the best drug rehab facility in the state. He secured his wheelchair in the reserved area at the front and as they drove he pondered his limited options. In the past suppressing his feelings had been easier. He had trained himself not to want things. Was that because somewhere inside he had always felt unworthy of them?

Could you even grow up in a society that cared about achievement, productivity, and working yourself into the ground without feeling your disabled body made you useless? These were thoughts he had tried so hard not to think, always pushing them down and reminding himself to be grateful for all he had. Even knowing there were people who used him as the worst case scenario in their own minds, grateful not to be like him.

The bus wove further and further through thickly wooded hills as Dylan's thoughts became darker and darker.

It wasn't often talked about but in the world of disability there were still haves and have-nots. A hierarchy some people called it. Dylan was somewhere in the middle, able to care for himself independently but missing a lot of the key aspects everyone mentioned when it came to attractiveness. No one ever said they were looking for a small man with odd proportions. There were disabled men who got girls. The handsome, athletic, confident, former-military paraplegics. Those guys had experience to draw on and maybe some innate entitlement that born-disabled guys never had. Or was he just projecting his own insecurities? How did you even root out internalized ableism?

Stephanie had awakened something inside him that had been dormant a long time. He no longer wanted to put it back to sleep. Could he take what he had learned from their relationship to do better the next time? Would the experience he had gained help him make the first move for the next girl?

But he didn't want another girl. He wanted her. There was no substitute for Stephanie. He didn't know if that was realistic. More likely David was right and, if his brother went through with what he had threatened, probably Dylan would be seeing him on her YouTube channel before long.

The bus groaned to a stop on Main Street of a quaint little town. This was as far as it went. Dylan waited for the driver to start the lift and then he was deposited on a cobblestone sidewalk and the bus drove away, looking out of place in this fairytale town. Adorable but also annoying. The cobblestones rattled his teeth as he tried to navigate the sidewalk and his stomach lurched with fear each time he dipped or bounced. The sidewalk was narrow and Dylan moved slowly, afraid he could tumble into the street at any moment.

He knew where the rehab facility was from when they had dropped their mother off a month ago but he hadn't been back since. A little guilt nibbled on his insides. Maybe he should have sought out her advice far sooner. In trying to protect her he had missed out on so much. His own mother, the only family he and David had, and they had kept even her in the dark.

This town was also on a hill and by the time Dylan arrived at his destination he was exhausted and his arms and shoulders ached. Luckily, the facility itself was as accessible as a hospital. The doors parted as Dylan wheeled through the wide front entrance to a reception desk that wasn't absurdly high. He gave the name they had checked their mother in under, not wanting to use *Sinclair* just in case of media attention.

He was ushered out the back of the building to a smooth stone patio with a view of a river. Trees shaded the benches around the outside edge of the patio. No one else was there today. Dylan parked himself towards the back where he could most clearly see the gentle river winking in and out between stones.

"Hi, sweetie."

He turned one wheel and saw his mother was walking over to the bench next to him. He smiled. "You look good," he said. "Healthy."

She nodded. "Thank you."

There was a gauntness to her face that would probably never fill in but she had gained some weight and she looked less ghost-like. She lit a cigarette and they both looked out to the forest and river quietly for a few minutes.

Finally Dylan said, "There's something I want to talk to you about, mom."

"I'm here."

He wondered how long she had been waiting to say those words. It had been a long time since Dylan or David had even tried to rely on her for anything. He knew that she wanted to make up for the past but they had all gotten used to not leaning on her for anything.

"This whole music thing," he continued, "All these years it's been me. It's my voice people are in love with."

His mother nodded, a sad smile playing on her lips. "I know," she said.

That was the last thing Dylan had expected her to say. "You do?"

"Your brother can't carry a tune to save his life. You think I don't know that? What I've never understood is why you let him take your spotlight." She reached out and touched her fingers to his cheek, a gesture so full of affection that he almost started crying.

"I had to do whatever it took to make it successful," he said. "People reject me but they never reject David."

There was a pause, his mother looking at him seriously, the cigarette burning forgotten between her fingers. "Dylan," she said looking directly in his eyes, "your father didn't reject you. He never even knew you. He missed out on knowing his son and that was his problem, not yours."

Dylan looked down at his lap, avoiding her penetrating gaze. "I just wanted to make it better," he said quietly, "for you and for David. To replace what you lost."

"Oh honey." She snuffed out the cigarette in a nearby ashtray and reached over to squeeze his hands that were resting on his lap. "It's not your job to fix that. You have your own life to live and it would be a true tragedy to waste it trying to undo the past. I don't want that for you. I want to see you thrive and experience everything the world has to offer. I'm so sorry if my struggles have made that hard for you to do. I never want you to feel responsible for my life."

He didn't say anything and she continued, "I've made so, so many mistakes. And those mistakes are still hurting you. The only atonement I can make is to see you free yourself from trying to save me and choose your own life. I'll stay clean this time. I'll do whatever it takes so you don't feel like you need to rescue me. And in return you say yes to what you really want. Deal?"

"Deal," he said and she squeezed his hands again before sitting back on the bench.

"Dylan, what made you want to confess all this to me today after all this time? Did something happen?"

He glanced back at her. "Do mothers always know?"

"Yes," she said and waited for him to continue.

"I met a girl."

His mother gasped and her face lit up with delight. "Oh sweetie, that's wonderful. Tell me everything."

"She's beautiful and smart and driven. Around her it feels like you can do anything. She loves the same music I do and she saw me. Really saw me."

"I'm so happy for you."

"But she broke up with me."

"That bitch."

"Mom, please. I don't blame her. Honestly. She thinks I'm not trying hard enough and by the time I told her the truth, she didn't believe me. I just don't know what to do. I painted myself into a corner by asking David to take the credit for my work. I thought I could keep this going forever. I thought I would be okay with settling for less of a life if it meant protecting you. But there's so much life left and I'm already sick of it. What do you think I should do?"

"Win her back, of course. You can't spend the rest of your life being David's shadow and scapegoat. I want more for you and I'm your mother so you have to listen to me."

"What if it ruins everything we have? What if everything I built collapses?" he whispered. The late afternoon sunlight cast a golden glow over his mother and for a moment she looked like a Madonna in a painting. Visiting time would be over soon.

"Listen to me, my sweet baby boy, following your heart can't ruin something that isn't already destined to be ruined. If you pass up this moment, you're going to spend the rest of your life being eaten alive by regret. I know what I'm talking about. Go get that girl and tell her the truth. You've carried this secret far too long."

An orderly appeared in the doorway beaconing them back inside. Before they parted, his mother squeezed Dylan's shoulder and said, "Promise me you'll follow your heart."

He nodded. "I promise."

22

—·—

Stephanie stopped what she was doing and pulled off her headphones. She hadn't been wrong, there was a sound in her hallway. Someone was playing music. That had never happened before. It was always her playing the music. She stood up and moved closer to the door. It had the distinctive breathy quality of David Sinclair's voice. She wished there was a peephole in her door although there was only one person who was likely to be playing a David Sinclair song outside her door.

She got even closer to the door trying to figure out what the song was. It was more acoustic than she was used to from David. Wait, even stranger it was a 90s song. One of her favorites. When had David recorded this?

Even though she was still angry at Dylan she yanked open the door. And whatever words she had been about to shout at him died in her mouth.

Dylan was sitting in front of her door, a guitar eclipsing most of his body, hugged against his chest, his fingers stroking the strings, and he was singing. As he crooned *Breakfast at Tiffany's,* he looked up from his guitar to meet her eyes.

"Oh my God," Stephanie whispered. Her knees buckled and she staggered back against her door frame for support. "It really is you."

His fingers stopped on the strings. He nodded. "Always has been," he said.

"I'm sorry I didn't believe you."

"I'm sorry I expected you to believe me without showing you."

For several moments they just stared at each other.

Then Stephanie stood back and said, "Do you want to come in?"

He shifted the guitar by its strap onto his back so he could wheel into her apartment, the door falling closed behind him.

"I should have trusted you. God, Dylan, I've missed you so much." Tears sprang to her eyes and she tried to blink them away.

He smiled and she couldn't hold back any longer. She dropped down to her knees and took his face in her hands, kissing his lips. His strong arms circled her shoulders.

There was so much to ask and to say but they couldn't stop kissing. Their physical need for each other was the most pressing thing right then. He slipped the guitar off his back and leaned it against the wall behind her door. They both headed for the bed at the same moment, though Stephanie got there first as wheeling over carpet was slow going. She watched his muscular shoulders and arms, anticipating the feel of them around her again.

She made space for him to heave his body onto the bed and then snuggled up against him, peppering kisses on his neck.

"Wait," Dylan said, looking her right in the eyes. "Before we go any further, I have to ask. Did my brother...?"

"Make a move on me?" She snorted. "Yeah."

"What happened?"

"I told him to take a hike." She made it sound like it had been easy to turn David down. In that moment had she been tempted? Not really. Despite what it could do for her she had felt an instant revulsion to his snake oil voice.

"Thank you," Dylan said, relief plain on his face.

"Hey, once you've had the real thing, bargain brand just won't do." She grinned and he pulled her on top of him turning her grin into a giggle.

Pushing aside just the bare minimum of clothing, Stephanie took his cock in her hand and rubbed the tip across her dripping pussy.

"There's a pill I can take," Dylan said softly. "It takes time to work, though."

"No need," she said. She worked the shaft hard with her hand and increased blood flow began to stiffen it until she could slide it inside with a satisfied little sigh. No condom this time. Now that she knew he had only ever slept with her and his body didn't even ejaculate, she was no longer worried about it.

She rocked her hips and slammed his rapidly deflating dick against the back of her vagina. As it softened, the cock became wider, filling her in a new and different way. Dylan meanwhile started using his fingers on her clit, his long arms making it easy to reach. She looked into his eyes that had become dark with desire and hunger for her.

It sent her over the edge and she shivered as waves of release crashed through her. She collapsed back down beside him and they lay side by side in Stephanie's bed again, she on the side against the wall and his chair next to her bedside table as before. As though it belonged there.

They both adjusted their clothes and then Dylan said, "Okay, I know you're dying of curiosity. Go ahead, ask me anything."

"How did it happen? And how have you been pulling it off all these years?"

"The radio execs liked the music but I'm no heartthrob. The best I was going to be was a viral clip from America's Got Talent and a couple appearances on Ellen. A novelty. I figured if Milli Vanilli could do it, so could we. They went for the idea."

"You were the one who suggested substituting David for you?"

Dylan nodded. "We each have our strengths," he said.

"And confidence ain't yours," Stephanie sighed.

Dylan laughed darkly. "My confidence never stood a chance." He took a deep breath and then said, "You asked about my parents but I never told you. So here's the truth. My father abandoned us because he couldn't handle having a disabled son. Mom had to take on multiple jobs and the stress drove her to drugs. My whole life I was a burden and the reason we struggled as much as we did. And I was the reason David didn't have a father and Mom didn't have a partner. We all knew if not for me they would have had a much easier and nicer life. I wasn't going to blow a chance to do some good for my family."

For a moment Stephanie was at a loss for words. Whatever issues she may have with her family, it was nothing compared to the trauma Dylan had been through. She didn't even want to imagine little baby Dylan knowing that his family was breaking apart because of him. She shuddered and felt an overwhelming need to relieve him of the burden.

"Sounds more like they would have had a much easier and nicer life if your mother hadn't picked a douchebag to father her children. You had no control over being born with a disability. I mean, isn't that more on your mother? Aren't there vitamins mothers can take?"

"Been reading up on spina bifida?"

"Maybe."

"It's not easy on a family. And it's expensive to have a disabled child. I don't blame them for the choices they made."

"Well I do," Stephanie said with a huff.

Then her eyes landed on her computer and suddenly it hit her. This was what she had been waiting for. The scoop of the decade and a story no one else had. This was the opportunity she had been waiting years for.

She bolted upright and eagerly said, "You've got to let me do a video on this for my channel. Imagine the attention!"

"No, absolutely not. Did you not hear what I just told you? This farce is what's saving my family."

"Dylan, you did it. You saved your family and now just think what this could mean for me. You could save me from my hellhole of a job."

Dylan pushed himself up to sitting too. "What happens if your channel doesn't succeed?" he asked.

"It breaks my heart and I live a miserable life." Visions of being Marcus's perfect domestic servant floated through her mind.

"But you don't wonder if you'll have a home. Or if you'll be able to eat."

That brought her up short. He was right. She had a safety net and he did not. But it was hard to understand where he was coming from when he now had more money than he knew what to do with. And the opportunity to help her was *right there*.

"Okay, but you don't really think you're going to pull this off forever, right? The truth will come out at some point. Why shouldn't it benefit me when it does?"

"That's why you're really here, isn't it? That's the reason you've been with me. All to further your career."

"Dylan, come on. That's not fair."

"Isn't it, though? Why would a beautiful woman go out with me? Everyone has been asking that question and now I know the real answer. It's what they suspected all along. I wanted to believe that there was a girl out there who would see the real me and not care about my body. But that's just too much to ask for, as it turns out."

"Do you think that little of me? How dare you suggest I've been faking it all along. I slept with you!"

"I don't have to subject myself to this. I'm leaving." He pushed his legs over the side of the bed.

"You will listen to me," Stephanie insisted and before he could grab his wheelchair she shoved it out of his reach. With the force she used it rolled clear across the floor despite the carpet and bumped against her bathroom door.

She realized her error immediately but it was already too late. The look of betrayal on his face was heartbreaking and she felt her gut wrench.

"I'm so sorry," she said, rushing to retrieve the wheelchair.

He was already gripping the bedside table tightly and easing his body onto the floor, preparing to leave with or without his chair.

"Dylan please," she said. He said nothing as she relinquished her grip on the wheelchair in front of him. He didn't look at her as he grabbed the frame and seat of the chair and slowly, painstakingly hoisted himself back onto it. Stephanie gripped her own arms, digging her fingernails in to stop herself from trying to help. He was shaking so hard he could barely move and his breath came in ragged bursts. Hands trembling, Dylan slowly made his way to the door and left without looking at her.

As soon as he was gone and the door clicked shut behind him Stephanie sank to the floor, face in her hands. How had their reconciliation lasted such a brief moment? She hadn't meant to take his wheelchair away. She just wanted him to listen. All the hope and happiness of a moment ago evaporated instantly.

This was really it. There was no coming back from taking a wheelchair away from a disabled man. There weren't even any words for the kind of monster who would do that. All the time she spent wishing she could get him back and that the problem of his lack of ambition would be magically solved and then when it actually happened, she ruined it instantly.

The chance to get what she wanted for her career at last was just too tempting. How could he blame her for that? Had he forgotten what it felt like to be trapped in a bad situation?

Then she noticed he had left his guitar leaning against her wall. Maybe she would still have the opportunity to apologize again once he calmed down. It would be an excuse to stop by his place in a few days.

She tried to burn frustrated energy cleaning around her apartment. She threw a soda can violently into the bin while cursing herself. She had work she could be doing. She stared at her laptop and thought about revealing the truth about David Sinclair anyway. The idea felt horrible. It wasn't her secret to reveal. She couldn't stand the thought of hurting Dylan again.

He might never know what she was sacrificing because of him but she wouldn't publish the story. She would keep on burning the candle at both ends, slowly dying from grant proposals. If she lost this job she would get another. But if someone else ended up breaking this story she wasn't sure how she would survive. The thought of that was almost enough to stop her breath.

Why did things have to be so complicated between them? Couldn't she have just met a nice random dude to fall for? Why did it have to feel like one of them was always losing no matter what they did?

She opened the door to bring the trash down the hall to the chute and stopped short when she saw Dylan still sitting in the hallway. He gave her a sheepish look. "My phone died," he said, holding it up and showing her the dark screen. "I can't reach my buddy who brought me up here."

She dropped the trash bag.

"Dylan, I'm so sorry."

His face was pale. Paler than usual. "That was really shitty what you did."

"I know," she whispered. "I wasn't thinking. I just wanted you to listen."

"There's no excuse for using your power against me like that."

"No, there's not." Stephanie had to wonder if this was the first time she had ever been the one with power in a situation. It was a bit surreal to have more power than a cis hetero white man.

"It may be unspoken but obviously we both know that I'm...vulnerable." He choked on the word. "How can I trust you when you could do something to take advantage of my weaknesses like that?"

Stephanie swallowed hard. She actually did have an answer to that. "Because I love you," she said, feeling like she was stepping off a cliff into empty air. This was as vulnerable as she could be, fully aware that it was the least likely time to get an "I love you" back but saying it anyway. Because it was true.

He blinked. He hadn't expected that answer. His face was full of fear and hope. She could see he wanted to believe it but he was scared.

"I swear," Stephanie said. "I will never touch your chair without your consent ever again. It was a terrible mistake. I love you and I promise that I will always respect you and your autonomy. Please forgive me." A tear spilled down her cheek and dropped from her chin.

"I love you too," he said quietly.

"Please come back inside," Stephanie said. "I won't ask again about doing videos on David. I'll find another direction. I respect your decision."

He looked at the open doorway behind her. She knew he was low on choices. He could keep sitting out here indefinitely, he could ask her to carry him down the stairs, or he could come back inside. The last thing she wanted to do right now was make him feel any more vulnerable than he already did.

"Do you want to call David from my phone?" she asked at last. "I assume you know his number."

He bit his lip for a moment then he nodded.

"Okay." She went back inside to grab her phone and brought it back out to him.

"He's not going to answer a number he doesn't know so I'll try texting him." His fingers tapped across the keyboard. Then they both stood there in silence waiting. Eventually Dylan handed the phone back. "He's going to send someone. If he came himself there would be a mob of paparazzi."

"Fair enough," Stephanie said. "Would you like me to get your guitar?"

"Yeah, that would be helpful. Thank you."

The ease they once had together was nowhere to be found. It was awkward and stiff between them. Stephanie retrieved the instrument, pausing behind the door to take some deep breaths and get control over her emotions.

When she came back she found the silent, hulking Shawn holding Dylan over his shoulder and the wheelchair in his other hand. So much for not making him feel more vulnerable. Dylan wasn't facing her but Shawn grunted and beckoned her closer, adding the guitar to his load.

"I'll text you," Stephanie said but Shawn was already carrying Dylan away down the stairs.

23

—•—

Dylan closed his eyes and let the humiliation wash over him. What choice did he have? Shawn wasn't one to appreciate the subtleties of how being carried like a piece of luggage in front of a hot girl might be something Dylan would prefer to avoid.

Some genius idea that had been to win her back. Music outside the window is supposed to be a no-fail maneuver, isn't it? He hadn't actually ever seen that movie. Now instead of wowing her with the revelation of his actual talent, he had fulfilled at least three of his top five fears in one go. He couldn't wait to just get home and try to forget this entire evening.

When Shawn deposited him at the car Dylan was startled to find that David was sitting in the back seat already. Dylan couldn't read his expression.

"Thanks for the rescue," Dylan said as he piled wheelchair pieces in front of his legs.

"We have a good thing going on here, Dylan." David said. "If you tell that girl the truth, you screw it up."

"Maybe I'm ready to screw it up."

David's eyes narrowed. "You have no idea what you're asking for," he said.

"Oh come off it, you just love all the attention."

David looked out the window instead of at Dylan as he said, "It used to be fun. Now it's just exhausting. Never being able to go anywhere without it being a huge fucking deal is not as fun as it looks and you, little brother, would hate it."

He probably would hate it. He had never really wanted to be the face of the brand. But that wasn't the point. "If you're tired of it, then let's stop," Dylan said.

"And how fast will we be right back where we started? With nothing? I know you understand that this isn't just your secret. We finally just got mom out of that shithole and the rehab place is not cheap."

He wasn't wrong. Telling Stephanie was a huge risk. And now that she knew, there was no telling what she would do with the information. She could easily still release the story whether he wanted her to or not. He had given up the control he had over his secret. And for what?

To impress a beautiful woman. To try to prove that he was worthy of her.

Was that really worth the risk of losing the resources to help their mother? Was it worth the risk to everything he had spent his life building? Sure their mother thought so but she wasn't exactly known for making the best decisions.

Dylan had pulled his family out of poverty. Nearly single-handedly. Couldn't he just appreciate that without people needing to know? Or rather needing one person in particular to know. He didn't mind the whole world looking at him like he was a worthless waste of space if just Stephanie knew what he had really accomplished.

And now she did. So whatever came next, Dylan was just going to be at peace with it. Whether he heard from her again or not, he had done everything he could to take control of his life and he could live with that. He didn't know where they stood after this rollercoaster of an evening but she had said she loved him so there was hope for them yet.

David was looking down at his phone now and he didn't say anything else. They went back to their respective homes in silence.

***

When Dylan woke up the next day he had a text from Stephanie. It said *I have an idea*. When he asked what it was, his phone started ringing.

"What's up?" he asked, putting the phone on his bedside table with the speaker on.

"I was thinking," Stephanie said, her disembodied voice sounding far away and small, "What you did coming over here yesterday was really brave." Before he could say anything she continued. "It made me realize that I've played it safe and I haven't put myself out there for you the way you did for me."

Dylan rubbed his eyes. "What are you saying?"

"I want you to meet my family."

If he had been holding the phone he would have dropped it. Every muscle he could control instantly tensed. He had already met her brother and that had gone horribly. But it wasn't like he could date her and never be introduced to her parents. He felt like he was going to be sick.

She continued, "If we're going to do this again, we're going to do it right. No hiding, no secrets. I'm done with living two separate lives. You are coming into my world."

Even though he was terrified, he wasn't going to lose her again. "Deal," he said. He already knew they didn't approve of him and was there anything he could actually do to change their minds? He couldn't exactly be not white or be not disabled. Maybe he could get some pointers from Keenan about meeting a Black family.

"Every Sunday we go to church together and then have dinner at my parents' house. Will you come with me this weekend?"

"*This* weekend?" He didn't have any excuse not to and she knew it.

"Please say yes," Stephanie said. "I want to tell them that I choose you."

"When you put it like that, how could I refuse?"

"I'll pick you up Sunday morning!"

He hung up and stared up at the ceiling. The image of Adam bursting through Stephanie's apartment door came immediately to his mind. The last thing Dylan wanted to do was see that guy again. Was Stephanie's brother still angry? Was he going to make things super uncomfortable for Dylan? Try to drive him off? Well, whatever happened Dylan was going to do what it took to not lose Stephanie again.

24

B right and early Sunday morning Stephanie was at Dylan's house
with her little red car. Lisa was right, she shouldn't have been hiding
him. She loved him, she was proud of him, and she wasn't going to pretend
otherwise any longer. You couldn't love someone and then be ashamed to
be seen with them. Stephanie was ready to think with her heart.

"Your hair!" Dylan blinked in shock as he got into the car.

Stephanie shook her head back and forth, the straight bob swishing
around her cheeks. "What do you think?"

"What did you do to it?"

"It's a wig. If you're going to date a Black girl, you're going to have to
get used to hair changes."

Stephanie noted that Dylan had followed her instructions to dress up.
He had on creased navy slacks, actual loafers, and a button down white
shirt with a navy tie. His jaw was clean shaven and his shaggy brown hair
was combed with gel.

"Wow, you clean up fine," she said.

He grinned. "Why, thank you," he said.

They started the drive to church and on the way, to calm their nerves,
Dylan told Stephanie stories about his life as a secret rock star: being

a fly on the wall at important meetings, watching David squirm when interviewers asked him about his inspiration for his lyrics, getting people's honest reactions to his work because they had no idea it was his.

As they pulled into the parking lot, Dylan grew quiet. She saw him watching through the window as gorgeous Black families dressed to the nines drifted towards the door like a kaleidoscope of butterflies.

"I probably should have mentioned earlier," Stephanie said. "My ex-boyfriend might be here."

"Oh great," Dylan muttered. "I can't believe I agreed to this. This is the worst idea you've ever had."

"You haven't even known me that long," Stephanie said.

"That's a little terrifying." He sighed and looked out the car window again. "We don't really have to do this, right? I'll just stay here in the car."

"You don't want to ever meet my family?"

"Well I mean couldn't we meet at a restaurant? I can be on the far side of the table. Less shocking."

Stephanie reached over and patted his leg. "Sweetie, that wouldn't help." She didn't have to say the obvious truth that he was short enough that it was immediately noticeable, not to mention the way he listed to the right. "Besides, they already know you use a wheelchair."

He didn't look reassured.

"Hey," Stephanie said, placing a hand on his knee even though he couldn't feel it. "We're in this together and we'll get through it together. Okay?"

He took a deep breath, then opened his car door and grabbed the wheelchair components from the back seat to reassemble beside the car.

Stephanie stood on her side waiting. He really did cut a handsome figure in his Sunday best. Dylan looked across the lawn. "I see your brother over there," he said. "Are those your parents with him?"

"Yep. And his wife, Gina. Come on."

They crossed the grass towards Stephanie's parents, Dylan pushing hard over the bumpy ground. She could see the tension in both her mother and father, watching with wary eyes as they approached.

"Mom, Dad, this is Dylan."

"Hello," her mother said stiffly. Her father said nothing, his face still as stone. But Dylan smiled good-naturedly and greeted them both. "It's an honor to meet you, sir, ma'am."

Her mother had a *don't embarrass us* expression on her face. For a moment no one said anything and people drifted past them into the church. The way her family was positioned, Dylan was mostly hidden.

It was Adam who broke the tension. He clapped Dylan on the shoulder and grinned. "Good to see you again, man."

Then Gina gave a shy smile and said, "Lovely to meet you."

"You too, thank you," Dylan said.

Stephanie shot her brother a grateful smile. She admired how adaptable Dylan was too. He was in a difficult situation but he surrendered to it and went with the flow.

"Well, let's go in," her mother said with a resigned sigh.

"We'll meet you there," Stephanie said. More quietly to Dylan she said, "The ramp is this way."

While the rest of her family went up the front steps, Stephanie and Dylan veered to the side and went up the ramp together. A satisfied glow warmed her core. She could really see this becoming her norm, going to church with her family and having Dylan by her side.

At the entrance to the church stood Marcus. As Stephanie looked at him she realized that she no longer had any romantic feelings for him. No butterflies and no nerves. He was a good man, she knew that, he just wasn't the right fit for her. She hoped he saw that too.

"Hey, Marcus. This is my boyfriend, Dylan."

The shock flashed behind his eyes for a moment but he didn't lose his cool. He held out his hand to Dylan and shook firm and hard. But Dylan was not easily intimidated and Stephanie could see he was matching Marcus's hand strength. There was a subtle competition that no one but Stephanie was a witness to.

It was Marcus who broke first, but he smiled in a way that told her Dylan had earned some of his respect. He nodded to the doorway and the three of them proceeded into the church.

As usual, there was a lot of movement. People milled around, some sitting but most still standing and talking with their friends. Stephanie wasn't a believer herself but she appreciated the community of her church family. Around white people there was always a subtle sense of putting on a bit of an act. Or maybe it was more like being on alert, her body sensing the possibility of danger. Here there was hardly ever a white person in sight.

If Dylan was feeling anything like that she couldn't tell. He seemed at peace, radiating the same calm energy that had drawn her to him in the first place.

The church main hall was filled with folding chairs rather than pews so it was simple to remove one for Dylan's wheelchair. Several people were craning their necks to look at him. He was certainly an oddity here in more ways than one.

As the service got started there was music and singing. Everyone was clapping and swaying in time. Not surprisingly Dylan kept up with the rhythm of the clapping perfectly. If anyone had been paying attention for it, his musical ability would be obvious. But no one here connected him to David.

After a rousing sermon the pastor announced a time for healing prayers and asked anyone seeking healing to come to the front. This wasn't something that happened every week and Stephanie hoped it wasn't inspired by seeing Dylan and assuming that's what he had come for. Aunt Sophie certainly seemed to think so.

Sophie leaped from her seat and took hold of Dylan's shoulders. "Healing prayers, come on now." She started pushing Dylan towards the front of the church.

"Wait, Auntie!" Stephanie hurried out of her seat.

But Dylan turned his head and gave Stephanie a small smile. "It's okay," he mouthed. She saw the surrender in his face. Whatever happened at church, he was just going to ride the wave. So she sat back down and watched Dylan get pushed into a line of people to be prayed over.

After the prayer Aunt Sophie pushed him back to their seats while the two of them chatted personably. It warmed Stephanie's heart to see his kindness with her Godmother.

Once the service ended, they lingered a while in the hall. Family friends came over to get a closer look at Stephanie's new man. One particularly bold uncle looked Dylan up and down and said, "So this is the white one, eh?"

Stephanie's father drew himself up to his full height. He may have finally accepted that he was not going to change Stephanie, that she would never fit into the box that had been drawn for her, and constantly fighting her was going to be an exhausting life. "That's right," he said. "And you gotta respect that he showed his pasty ass here to face all of us!"

The tone was jovial and everyone laughed.

"Balls of steel," the uncle said, nodding.

Dylan wisely kept his mouth shut and let everyone joke around him.

"So what's with the wheelchair? What happened to you?" another person said.

Stephanie wanted to rescue Dylan but she also couldn't be rude to the elders so she was in a bind but Dylan was still in the mindset of going with the flow and seemed to have turned off any feelings of offense.

"I had a pretty severe birth defect, so I was born disabled," he answered.

More questions flooded in until it was finally time to leave for dinner.

"Sorry it's not over yet," Stephanie said in the car. She had meant this experience to be a gesture that showed Dylan that she was never going to hide him again but she hadn't fully anticipated how draining it was going to be for both of them. This day was not exactly a gift for him.

"We'll get it all over within one day, at least," Dylan said. "Everything from here on out will be easy."

"For sure." They drove out to Stephanie's parents house and parked in the driveway. Stephanie saw Dylan eyeing the steps to the front door that had no railing.

"You're really going to piggyback me up the stairs?"

Stephanie shrugged. "What other option do we have?"

Dylan groaned. "I changed my mind," he muttered. "I'm going to be a monk."

Stephanie acknowledged the joke with a smile but she said, "I know today has been challenging. And I want you to know I'm super grateful that you're handling my family with so much grace."

"Pulling out the flattery?" He raised an eyebrow.

"I'm serious."

"I know." He smiled.

After some strategizing, Stephanie brought the wheelchair to the door first and then came back to the car to kneel down and let Dylan shift himself onto her back. She lifted him up and carried him up to the porch and back to his chair. They were already well practiced with the piggyback method by now and it went perfectly smoothly. As far as they could tell there was no audience to the maneuver, though someone could have been watching through a window.

Stephanie held open the squeaky screen door and the moment Dylan popped a wheelie up over the door frame, Nessie came bounding down the hallway, her toenails clacking frantically on the floor, and put her paws on Dylan's lap. She eagerly reached her tongue for his face.

"Nessie! Down!" Stephanie said, trying to wrestle the dog off Dylan. But he took Nessie's face in his hands and baby talked to her while scritching behind her ears. She was in absolute heaven.

"Is there anyone you can't charm?" Stephanie asked and Dylan chuckled.

Long ago, when she had first looked at the magazine article about the Sinclair brothers, she had pegged David as the charismatic one. Now she could see they each possessed their own unique kind of charisma. And while David's left a bitter aftertaste, Dylan's was all sweet.

They made their way to the dining room and Stephanie moved aside a chair for Dylan. They were heavy solid wood chairs and she doubted Dylan would be able to pull one without more leverage. At the house things were quieter than church. Her parents were here and Adam and Gina plus Aunt Sophie but that was it.

Sophie and Dylan seemed to be becoming fast friends. Dinner was enjoyable mainly because Dylan asked Sophie all the right questions to get her telling stories about her youth as the first professional Black ballet dancer in the city's company. Stories came out that Stephanie had never heard. She noticed a look of pride on her mother's face as she listened. It was the most fun family dinner had been in years.

After eating they all moved to the living room.

"Stephanie, can I talk to you over here?" Her mother guided her to a quiet corner. Stephanie looked over to Dylan but he looked fine talking with Sophie so she let herself be led away.

"It's nothing against him," her mother said in a low voice. "But I'm concerned because I don't want you to tie yourself to someone you'll have to take care of."

"He doesn't need that, mom. He's very independent."

"For now. But what happens as his body deteriorates? You're signing yourself up for a very challenging life if you choose him."

Her mother's reasoning made no sense to Stephanie. It just wasn't how she thought. "I can't make choices based on fears about what could happen. Any of us could have our body deteriorate."

Her mother sighed. "The confidence of youth. Okay, I just needed to say my piece. Now come with me to sort what you want to keep from the attic."

***

Dylan watched Stephanie ascend the stairs with her mother and tried not to worry that somehow Stephanie would be talked out of love with him. Sophie had gone to get another plate so he had no distraction from wondering what was happening upstairs.

At that moment Adam came over and sat down on the bottom step facing him. Dylan's stomach tensed. He couldn't help but think of the moment Adam walked in on him and Stephanie in bed and now Stephanie was out of sight, so there was no telling what Adam might say having him alone. Dylan didn't have a sister but he understood that brothers got protective. Was this a coordinated plan to scare him off?

"Listen, man," Adam said, "I shouldn't have reacted like that. You're a good dude and I was just protecting my sister, you know? I'm sorry it caused all this ruckus."

Of all the things Adam could have said that was not what Dylan had anticipated. It took a moment to recover from the shock enough to answer. "I appreciate that. I know I'm no one's first choice for their sister to be with."

"Hey now, she loves you and she told me the way you defended her. That takes some serious balls to stand up to racists. Oh I mean, not stand up but you know."

"Figurative standing, I got it."

"Yeah, so as long as you treat Stephanie right and make her happy, we don't have a problem."

"Thank you."

There was a brief pause and then Adam said, "So are you really David Sinclair's brother?"

Dylan laughed. "Yes, he's my older brother."

"That's cool. Never would have thought Stephanie's hobby would actually connect her with a famous person. Amazing." He stood and walked away shaking his head.

Stephanie descended the stairs a few minutes later. At first he thought she was going to rest her hand on his shoulder but she stopped herself, cognizant of her family watching.

At last they were able to leave. It was already dark outside. Dylan slumped in the passenger seat and closed his eyes.

"You were amazing in there," Stephanie said. She continued, "I have another idea."

Dylan opened his eyes again. "I'm not sure I can take any more of your ideas," he said.

"To make up for tonight I thought you might want to join me and Lisa and Chance at our movie night at my place. You and Lisa seemed to really get along."

"Yeah, Lisa is awesome. I'd love to." That sounded like a much more enjoyable evening. Although he was glad he had faced meeting her family. The unknown was always scarier and they seemed to be reluctantly accepting that there was no stopping Stephanie from doing what she wanted. He really couldn't have asked for it to go any better than that.

25

"Stephanie Rowe report to conference room 1," a voice came over the intercom at the office.

Stephanie and Betsey exchanged glances. There was no meeting scheduled. The anxiety hit Stephanie's stomach and she almost thought she might throw up. She got shakily to her feet and walked towards conference room one feeling like she was walking to the guillotine. Or more accurately, the firing squad.

When she opened the door, the only other people there were Bolan and someone she recognized from HR.

"Stephanie, have a seat," Bolan said. He looked like he was struggling to suppress a smile. The bastard. He had been looking forward to this day since she started at the company.

It was layoffs and he could have just diplomatically said her role wasn't needed or something like that. Instead he detailed everything he disliked about her. She was lazy, insubordinate, and coasting on a paycheck. Even HR tried to shush him.

"Do you agree that you have been terrible at this job?" Bolan demanded.

Some of it was deserved. Stephanie knew she wasn't working as hard as she used to. The thing was, there's only so long you can work your butt off with no reward before you lose all motivation and just start doing the bare minimum. When she first started she was passionate and worked extra hard. But it never mattered.

"I don't agree," she said. She wasn't going to give him the satisfaction.

Bolan waited a beat but she didn't crack so he sighed and said, "You can go and clear out your desk."

She wanted to yell at him and call him a racist but in her heart she knew it would only further drive home his prejudice and make him think he was right about her. At least she didn't cry or betray her panic. She nodded calmly and stood to leave.

Back at her desk, Betsey looked up hopefully as Stephanie approached but Stephanie shook her head. "On to better things, I guess," Stephanie said.

"I'm so sorry," Betsey said, but she was glancing down the hall to make sure Bolan wasn't watching.

Before getting on her bicycle, Stephanie texted Dylan to tell him that she had lost her job. *Thank goodness I have movie night to look forward to tonight,* she wrote.

By the time she got home there was a reply. *I'm sorry, how are you feeling? Will you come over?* Stephanie wrote back.

There was a long pause before his reply came back. She started to panic a little. She needed him, he was going to be here for her, right?

The only way I can get to you quickly is if you come pick me up. I'll learn to drive, I promise.

Oh. She didn't really feel like driving but she did want Dylan here with her so she texted that she was on her way.

As he pulled his legs into the car he said, "Nothing to make you feel more like a burden than not being able to get to your girlfriend when she needs you."

She shrugged. "It is what it is."

"At least this is fixable," he said. "I can learn to drive and I can afford to get a car with hand controls. I'll make it a priority."

"Thank you," Stephanie said.

"Let me guess, it was that jerk Bolan."

Stephanie nodded. "He finally convinced management that I suck."

"What an ass."

"I can't say it was entirely undeserved. It's been hard to care about the work."

The city whirled by around them as Stephanie drove.

"He was trying to get you to quit so they wouldn't have to pay unemployment," Dylan said.

"Oh. That makes sense."

"So you did great and you'll be able to get some money to help you out."

She stopped the car in front of her parking spot for him to get out then joined him going up the ramp into the building. He strapped himself to the wheelchair and took hold of the railing with one hand, Stephanie just behind him. While pulling off this maneuver he was too winded to speak so they went up the stairs in silence, the only sound the clack of his caster wheels hitting each step. An old woman came down on the other side of the stairs and her jaw dropped but Dylan couldn't break his concentration so only Stephanie saw.

At the top Dylan said, "I want to help, so let me help. I have the money and I may as well spend it on you."

Stephanie considered as they walked down the hallway. Being stubborn about this was shooting herself in the foot and probably offending him too. So she nodded.

"Okay," she said, "Maybe a loan to get me through until I can find another job?"

"Done. Absolutely. I'm sorry I can't do more."

He could do more, though. The thought popped into her head like a thread that kept coming loose no matter how you tied it. He was choosing not to help in the way that she actually wanted. But no, she had promised to keep her relationship separate from her work life. David's unwelcome voice came into her head "I hope you don't grow to resent him." She pushed the voice down and focused on the here and now. She was going to be content with his decision and take the help that he was offering.

At her apartment, they lay together in bed and strategized a plan for the coming months. What jobs Stephanie would look for, what tasks to prioritize in getting ready to apply. The time passed quickly and pretty soon there was a knock at the door.

Stephanie got up to open it while Dylan got back into his chair. Tiny ran to Dylan and began eagerly sniffing him.

"Great to see you again!" Lisa said. "I brought IPAs in your honor." She handed the beer off to Stephanie and gave Dylan a hug.

Once Lisa stood back up, Tiny judged the distance and then leapt right up into Dylan's lap.

"Oh my God, I'm so sorry," Lisa said, shooing at the dog.

"No worries," Dylan said, stroking Tiny's head. "Tell me about the little guy."

Lisa sat down and happily told Dylan all about her beloved dog while Stephanie got the movie set up.

When Chance arrived he hesitated in the doorway and frowned on seeing Dylan. He came in and didn't greet him but went straight to getting a bowl to pour popcorn into without a word.

With Stephanie, Lisa, and Chance on the floor Dylan was somewhat removed in his wheelchair so he lowered his body to the rug with everyone else. He had to lean against the bed to support himself. Stephanie curled up next to him, tucking her legs beneath her.

Chance was practically bristling and Stephanie couldn't figure out what was bothering him. She tried to focus on the movie but she couldn't help feeling the waves of negativity coming off her friend.

Even after the movie ended Chance was still unusually quiet.

Finally Stephanie snapped, "What is with you, Chance?"

"Can I see you out in the hall for a moment?" he said with a look that was supposed to mean something but Stephanie didn't know what.

Stephanie lightly closed the door behind them. "Why are you being such a grouch?"

"What you're doing is not right."

"What am I doing?"

He narrowed his eyes at her but she had no idea what he was talking about.

"You want me to ignore how convenient all of this works out for you. You get access to David by stringing along a vulnerable person. Frankly, it's disgusting."

"What?! He's not a fucking child, Chance."

"Children aren't the only vulnerable people. I'm not going to stand by and watch you exploit him. Call me when you come to your senses."

He strode away down the hall leaving Stephanie stunned. Is that what most people thought when they saw her and Dylan together? Would she always be fighting wild perceptions?

She went back into her apartment and leaned briefly against the closed door, sighing.

"Where's Chance?" Lisa asked.

"He left," Stephanie said without elaborating.

Dylan frowned but didn't say anything.

She rejoined him on the floor in front of the bed and they enjoyed the rest of the evening with Lisa and Tiny.

26

—·—

On Saturday Stephanie's phone buzzed in her pocket and when she pulled it out she saw a text from Dylan.

Meet me at Spotlight at 7:00. Make sure your phone is charged up.

That was a karaoke bar. What was he up to? There was no way he was going to let anyone in public hear him sing. Nor was there any chance Stephanie would be singing in public. But if there was one thing the ups and downs of the last months had taught her it was to trust Dylan.

So she smoothed her hair into two afro puffs, changed into a fresh t-shirt and headed for her car.

Being a Saturday night the bar was relatively full but not packed. She saw Dylan sitting in his wheelchair next to one of the tables closest to the door and as she approached, he said, "Turn on your livestream."

"What is going on, Dylan?"

His face was deadly calm as he nodded behind her.

There was a sound by the door just as Stephanie turned to see David in the doorway, his regular entourage just behind him. She lifted up her phone and started streaming to YouTube. At first David didn't see them and as his eyes took in the karaoke stage his face turned ashen.

He tried to back out, nearly tripping over his friends. But he had been seen. Whispers around them rose into cheers and clapping. David was trying to smile but there was a terror behind his eyes that Stephanie had never seen before. He looked around desperately until his eyes found Dylan.

Through the camera view of her phone Stephanie watched them exchange a cryptic look and then a sudden calm resignation came over David's features. His usual roguish charm was back and he smiled for the fans, raising his hands and playing into the excitement. Whoops and cheers went up again. People eagerly guided David to the stage and pressed a microphone into his hand. He grinned, getting into the spirit.

The DJ put on a track that was a classic David Sinclair. More people had their phones out now but Stephanie had the audience for a livestream like this.

Over the din and cheering at first no one could hear David singing. He crooned into the microphone, his handsome face shadowed in dim lights. Stephanie looked at Dylan who was sitting completely still watching David with no expression on his face. She knew that he had crafted this moment, ready at last to emerge from the background of life.

Slowly David's voice began to be audible over the excitement. This was a voice none of them had heard before, not even Stephanie. It was shaky and broken. People looked at one another, confusion taking over. Was this a joke?

But David was a picture of complete sincerity. It was the most honest Stephanie had ever seen him. He poured his heart into the song but it was very clear that he was tone deaf.

The room had fallen nearly silent as David sang on. His eyes burned with an angry fire as he looked at each onlooker. Then his eyes met Dylan's and he stopped singing, a small smile playing on his lips. He beckoned to his brother, who rolled closer to the stage.

David knelt down and passed the microphone to Dylan, stretching the cord to reach. The track continued to play but all other sound had ceased. Stephanie panned the crowd, all of them riveted with shock.

In the next beat Dylan began to sing and David's famous voice emerged from his mouth. Stephanie held up the camera but she watched without the lens as her boyfriend took back what was his.

Her chest tightened with pride. She could hear gasps behind her but she was focused on only him. He looked directly at her as he sang and his face was a study in pure joy.

David leaned back in a chair at the table where Stephanie and Dylan had been and watched. By now every person in the bar had their phone out. Stephanie wished she could check Twitter at the same time but dared not stop the stream.

The song finished and no one knew how to react. There were a few scattered claps but mostly people were looking at each other confused. Dylan handed back the microphone to the man in charge and glided back over to the table where Stephanie and David were waiting. David seemed at peace, resigned that it was all out of his control now. "Well," he said, pressing his hands on the table as he stood up, "I think I have some lawyers to talk to about us breaching a contract. Catch you two love birds later."

David, Shawn, and Keenan left and then a few people began to approach Dylan and Stephanie. Stephanie held up her phone again. "Want to tell them what's going on?" she said.

Dylan nodded. As she recorded, he addressed the whole room. "Hey everyone. I'm David's brother, Dylan. I felt the time had come to stop lying to everyone and come clean about what we've been doing. I hope that you can forgive us in time. I asked David to pretend to be me and it's all gotten out of hand. Thank you and I'm sorry."

Looking at Stephanie he nodded his head towards the door. She put her phone away and they made their way to the exit.

"So what happens now?" Stephanie asked out on the sidewalk.

Dylan shrugged. He took her hands in his. "I don't know, "he said. "I'll do my best to keep my career going but here's what I think will happen. There will be a big surge, I'll be on all the talk shows, concerts sold out, music in commercials. The whole thing. And then something else will capture the public imagination and my career will drop like a stone in the ocean never to be heard from again. The novelty 15 minutes of fame I was trying to avoid."

"I'm sorry," Stephanie said, knowing that without her he would have kept this going for many more years.

"Nah," Dylan said. "It was right to tell the truth. I couldn't keep living in David's shadow. I'm glad you gave me the push to finally do it."

Stephanie's phone buzzed. She took back her hands and checked it. An email asking to use her video on Entertainment Tonight.

Stephanie smiled at Dylan. "Don't worry," she said, "I'll take care of you financially."

He laughed. "Touché."

27

Epilogue

Stephanie stood next to the stage with her video camera in her hands. She looked over to the scattered tables and she couldn't help chuckling seeing Adam and Gina trying so hard to be supportive. Her brother was sincere in his desire to make up for how he had reacted to Dylan. And she had to give it to him that when he wanted to amend for something, he went all in. He had attempted to dress casual with well fitted dark jeans but he also had on a button-down shirt. Gina looked equally out of place in a tailored shift dress and lace cardigan.

The air was thick with the smell of sweat and spilled beer. The lights were too bright, and the music was too loud. But Stephanie didn't care. She was focused on the man up on the stage.

Dylan was wearing his black leather jacket and jeans as usual. His floppy hair was mussed, and his eyes were bright with excitement. He was singing his heart out, and the crowd was eating it up.

Stephanie could feel the energy from the crowd pulsing through her. She raised her camera and started filming. She wanted to hold onto this moment forever. What a wild ride life could take you on. A year ago she could never have imagined that she would be here. It wasn't what she had envisioned and yet it was so much better than anything she had pictured.

Right now Dylan was a media darling, going on late night talk shows as he had predicted. And those same shows licensed Stephanie's footage of the infamous night so David's stoney face of realization played over and over haunting him.

But to his credit David was taking the whole thing in good spirits. He was dabbling in acting and he always had a cheeky remark for anyone trying to get under his skin about the fraud he and Dylan had perpetrated.

Whether Dylan's career continued to grow or he became what he feared, a quick novelty, they knew they would manage. Between the two of them they were always going to find a way to keep going. Having someone you knew would be on your side through thick and thin was more healing than Stephanie would have thought.

Lisa joined Adam and Gina and waved in Stephanie's direction. The people Stephanie could count on were all here. Sadly that no longer included Chance.

There were those who would never understand the love between Stephanie and Dylan. It had never been clearer to her that you couldn't ever know what it was like inside someone else's relationship. There would always be people eager to say that she must be cheating on him, that he couldn't possibly satisfy her, that she wanted money from him. But in the end it was their loss that they couldn't see past the superficial to the power of real love.

Through the camera lens Stephanie kept watching. She could see the joy on Dylan's face as he sang. He was in his element, and he was loving every minute of it. She would take credit for helping to make that happen. Affection wrapped itself around her heart.

Neither of them were the same people they had been that warm night out on the sidewalk tentatively exposing small vulnerabilities. But what had been set in motion the moment Dylan laid his coat down on the wet ground led them here to a life full of hope for the future and love that would only continue to grow.

***

Thank you for reading! If you enjoyed this book please leave a review on Goodreads or Amazon. It helps so much!

***To get a bonus scene of Stephanie meeting Dylan's mom* visit my website at**

https://ruthmadisonbooks.com/bonus

www.ingramcontent.com/pod-product-compliance
Lightning Source LLC
Chambersburg PA
CBHW060325260626
47160CB00007B/2684